PUNCH

BARBARA HENDERSON

pokey
hat

First published in 2017 by Pokey Hat

Pokey Hat is an imprint of Cranachan Publishing Limited

ISBN: 978-1-911279-23-5

eISBN: 978-1-911279-24-2

Cover illustration by Corinna Bahr

www.corinnabahr.com

www.cranachanpublishing.co.uk

@cranachanbooks

cranachan

For my parents, Wolfgang and Ursula Haas,
who gave me my first string puppet for Christmas
when I was nine, sparking a lifetime love of puppetry.

CONTENTS

CHAPTER 1

INVERNESS, 1889
THE MARKET AT NIGHT

'Phineas! PHINEAS!'

Hands the size of spades shake me roughly awake and I blink.

It's not quite ink black; not yet. What does he want now?

'PHINEAS, up on your feet!'

Blindly, I feel around for my cap beside the bed—I don't feel dressed without it. Uncle Ewan reaches down, pulls the rough woven blanket off me and turns away while I pull on my breeches and button my jerkin as fast as I can, without the light of a candle or a fire in the grate. Which there never is, in this room.

'WILL you hurry, boy!'

I have barely straightened up, and he leans down till he is nose to nose with me. I try not to think about the reek of ale which hits my face, as I expected it to.

'Listen, Phineas. I'm only going to say this once. Know

1

the Lawrie House on Castle Street? The big one—the architect's house?'

Still sleepy, I nod and pull my cap further down. As my eyes get used to the dark, I can tell there's blood on his breeches, on his apron, on his sleeves. There's blood on his shoes, too. Butcher's badge of honour.

'DO YOU?' He shakes me by the ears and I try to nod. 'I do, Uncle Ewan, sir. I do.'

He lets go.

'Mind, that order his maid collected today? She never took the sausages, and Mr Lawrie has got an important breakfast with his guests.'

In other words, Uncle Ewan didn't give the maid the whole order. With every second, I wake up a smidgeon more, and now I'm awake enough to begin to understand. 'But sir…'

'No answering back, Phineas, I've told you that before. Run over to the market; find the guard. It's young MacLennan tonight. Go to our stall; find the ice box. The sausages'll be in there. Wrap the parcel. Take it to the Lawrie house. Knock at the servants' entrance, but quietly. With a bit of luck someone'll hear you.'

Uncle Ewan's moustache has things stuck in it, but it's too dark to see what.

'Sir and what if…'

'Well, you can't leave fresh meat out there on the steps.

There's rats. If nobody answers, you'll just have to wait.'

With this, he stretches up to his full height—a giant in my tiny attic chamber—and raises his hand, casting a fuzzy moon-shadow against my stone wall. I do not linger long enough to find out where it would fall. Instead I dart out, stopping only briefly to tie the laces on my boots; my father's boots when he was alive. They are still a wee bit big, but I simply couldn't wait any longer. I stumble down the narrow servants' stair, only used by me and Miss Garrow, the stern housekeeper, pull on a scarf, even though it's June, and shoot out into the street. A kind of fear laps at my feet, but I fight my fright the only way I know.

Running.

Along the cobbled street. Not a hoof beat to be heard, no sellers, no carts, no trestles, no anything. I glance up at the sky. The clouds are low and dark, as if they are deliberately hiding the moon. But I can tell it's late. Eleven maybe? It stays light for so long this far north—but soon it will be properly dark. I run faster, towards the greedy waters of the river, and jump at a splash.

Otter?

Salmon?

Seal?

I don't know, and I don't care—as long as it isn't a ruffian. I turn up the collar of my jerkin, but the river fog still chills me as I creak across the Greig Street Bridge, looking right and left all the while. My breaths come ragged now and I allow myself a trot, slowing down to a walk. I'll need to go right round to the main gate. Where will the night guard be? Won't he ask questions? After all, a twelve-year old should probably not be out on the streets by himself this late. And I might have to explain all over that I'm not actually related to Butcher Finlayson, but that he is my guardian and I work for him. Young MacLennan is new. He won't remember me.

People never remember the delivery boys.

The gas lights are still on in the market.

I try the gate as quietly as possible and thankfully, it gives. Still unlocked. The pillars tower above me like giant clubs. Every few seconds, the light from the market goes a little dimmer—the night guard is extinguishing the gas lanterns one by one.

If I'm quick, I might be able to get the sausages from the stall while I can still see. I wriggle through the narrow gap in the gate rather than opening it wider and risking more noise. Lifting and placing my feet gently, the low growl from the grocer's dog startles me. It guards the stall at night.

I give it a wide berth. In the mornings, it wags his tail for me, but the market is a different place tonight. Tonight, I smell of butcher's blood. Tonight, I'm an enemy. A sneak. A thief, stealing into its territory.

In the near-complete darkness of our stall, I feel around for the ice box, pull the lever and reach inside with freezing fingers. The steps of the night guard become clearer, more distinct. Aha, that feels like sausages. I won't wrap them here—I'll take the paper with me, before the night guard locks the gate.

The steps come closer and a portion of the light goes out nearby. A vague humming tune mingles with the familiar aroma of the market: fish, meat, fruit, sweat. Will I call out? I might give him a fright if I do, and I've heard that young MacLennan's got quite a temper. Will I crouch down low so he doesn't notice me as he passes? Then I might make it out through the gate unnoticed. Yes, that's a better idea. Being locked in overnight; now that would be worse than anything. I'd rather not imagine what Uncle Ewan's spade hands would do if his sausages weren't delivered. Young MacLennan must never know I was here.

I fold myself down low next to some sacks and hold my breath as the young man passes, whistling and clinking his bundle of keys.

Until it happens: a rising growl.

'Curse you, stupid dog!' the guard mutters, but the dog barks and MacLennan backs away, loses his balance and steadies himself against the trestle table beside ours. It's not sturdy enough! The table gives way and slides against the wall, and the guard topples backwards after it. He clutches at everything and anything to break his fall. His hand finds the gas pipe as his lantern clatters to the floor.

A spare trestle, leaning upright against the wall, wobbles with the impact, swinging forwards, backwards and forwards again, before landing on top of him with a crash. There is a crunching sound and then a whoosh. Suddenly, before I can gather a single thought, a flame shoots into the air, flashing bright in the ghostly hall. Young MacLennan yelps loudly, and I scream, and *he* screams louder when he sees me, trapped as he is under the flaming wreckage. The broken pieces of wood beneath him are catching fire, too.

Finally, my brain and my limbs seem to communicate. I scramble upright and try to pull the table off him, but it's solid—and on fire. Trying to smother the flames with a spare apron doesn't work either; it's fierce already. MacLennan lies trapped beneath, his mouth welded into a silent scream. My own eyes must be as wide as his—he can only be a few years older than me, barely an adult himself. The smoke is building. Fire shoots and sprays from the broken gas pipe beside us, but I can't leave him. *Can I?*

No, I can't. I may be small-built for my age, but I take a firm hold of the smouldering corners of the trestle and tug with all my might. 'Push, MacLennan—I can't move it myself!' I hiss, through teeth clamped together in pain. My palms are melting, surely, but I don't let go, and the trapped guard manages to get a foot to the underside of the burning table. We feel it tip a little, but it falls back. MacLennan yelps in pain. Again, we pull and push, harder, and it tips again before it finally topples off with a crash, loud enough to be heard above the swoosh of the pipe and the roar of the flames. No time; not even to take a breath of relief.

'Out!' I cough, stretching a hand towards him and heaving until I have pulled him upright. He doesn't speak, but he seems to be able to stand. I support him as best as I can.

Crouching low beneath the smoke, we stagger towards the main gate. The fire spreads to Uncle Ewan's trestle, and then to the unit on the other side, as sparks rain across the hall. I turn around once more: Mrs Wetherspoon's confectionary stall looks like it's trading in fire—all the paper bags dance with flames. We reach the entrance, panting, and stumble into the street to heave fresh air into our stinging lungs.

The guard looks at me and draws a deep breath. To thank me, to shout for help, or both.

Or so I thought.

His eyes narrow; his brain is clearly working fast. 'Boy! WHAT HAVE YOU DONE?' His croaking voice echoes all down Academy Street. Louder, he repeats: 'WHAT HAVE YOU DONE, BOY? YOU'VE SET THE MARKET ON FIRE!'

Frozen, like a statue, my own voice dies in my throat as he begins to bang on doors. 'THE MARKET'S ON FIRE. FIRE! FIRE! THE BOY DID IT!'

PUNCH

Smoke belches out through the market entrance.
And me?
I turn and run.

CHAPTER 2

RUN, PHINEAS!

It's cold, really cold. Or maybe it's only the sweat running down my neck. *Away, away from here*, is all I can think.

Other voices start to mingle with the shouts of the night-guard. Bells begin to ring and faces appear at windows and doors as I speed along Academy Street, turn right along the High Street, towards the Town House and the Bridge. More and more people pour into the street and an orange glow has formed behind the roof-tops. Smoke-edged flames claw higher and higher and higher into the sky.

I find myself turning into Castle Street. Why do I do that? Oh yes, I know—the sausages are still tucked into my jerkin. It's not even a proper package—I never folded the paper as I should; it's all crumpled. And as the sky over the market turns gold and the pillar of fire—like in the bible stories—reaches up to heaven, I look away and make a perfectly folded parcel of sausages in my hands. There. Something I can control.

The Lawrie House is only a short way up from here, and

I slow down, walking against the stream of curious night wanderers, all heading to the market to see. I don't turn to see. I won't turn.

Turning round will make it true.

Staying low, I head to the servants' entrance. The Lawrie footman and the housekeeper stand in the street, watching, their eyes narrow as they smart from the smoke in the breeze.

I thrust the parcel into the housekeeper's hands. 'Sausages from Finlayson's,' I wheeze, and my voice doesn't even sound like mine at all. She accepts it without question and turns back to the footman. Does she not wonder why I'm here at this hour, delivering sausages?

Part of me longs to stand here and talk with them, about the orange devil-dance in the sky and about the new-fangled gas lights that have sent so many buildings up in flames. *The market. What will happen now to all the traders who depend on it?* I would love to talk as if none of this was anything to do with me.

The boy did it.

Run, Phineas!

Without a plan of any sort, I cross Castle Street and head up the grassy slope towards the dark Sheriff Court. The trees are high at the prison end, and the bushes dense. I can climb and not be seen. Nobody would venture to a cursed place, full of criminals, in the dead of night. Would they?

Horses' hoof beats ring out on distant cobbles—the first fire engines are beginning to arrive. Although I am hundreds of yards away, the sound carries across the town. The clanking of pails being passed from man to man, river to market. The screams of dismay whenever the fire finds a new, explosive thing to devour and stabs a new blade of sparks into the smoky sky.

Where now? I must not be seen!

At last I spot a tall pine. Although the needles scratch my face and hands with every upward move, I feel I somehow deserve it. Higher and higher I climb, until few buildings block my view and my stomach lurches. The whole market is burning, as if the devil himself had struck the match, and it seems that the firemen have given up saving it, instead pouring water on the buildings beside. I don't know why, but I arrange myself as comfortably as I can on the branch, leaning back on the trunk. Rustling and fluttering is all around me, and I feel for the restless birds: their world is all wrong.

But mine? My world is as wrong as can be.

Hypnotised by the fire, I banish all thoughts of tomorrow. I stay because I have nowhere to go. I'm silent because I have nothing to say and no-one to say it to.

Those crowds in the streets, the faces at every window, the line of guards, running from the prison towards town to help—it is nothing to do with me. I am just watching.

I am just…

A sob rips through my lungs and my vision blurs, a mix of smoke and despair; until more flutterings and rustlings disturb me and the trunk sways alarmingly. I hold my breath. There is no mistaking it.

Someone is climbing my tree.

Someone heavy.

I cling to the trunk as tight as I can and peer down, and my blood freezes.

Through the dense needled branches, I recognise the subtle stripes of a prisoner's clothes.

CHAPTER 3

THE RUFFIAN

Time stops. A minute ago, all that mattered was the blazing market. I couldn't imagine thinking about anything else. Now all that matters are the swaying branches and the heaves of the ruffian as he makes his way up the tree.

Towards me.

It's dark, save for the glow of the town, so his outline is blurred like an approaching shadow. He is fast for a grown-up. I take a deep breath.

'Don't come any closer!' I hiss downwards, adding "sir" (I don't know why). 'I… I have a weapon.'

'Dinnae be daft.' His voice is low and hoarse. 'Ye're only a boy!'

His hands reach for a branch above his head.

I clamber onto the branch above me.

He follows. Closer and closer.

My heart beats so hard it may burst through my meat-stained shirt.

He's going to reach my feet soon, and I can't go much

higher. As it is, the tree has begun to lean. There is only one thing I can do.

I swing myself from the branch I've been holding on to. I don't know how, but my mind has flooded with what I learned about Isaac Newton and gravity at the Raining's School before Uncle Ewan made me leave. Gravity is my only hope.

Time slows as I swish through the air, aiming to kick him as hard as I can. Head, shoulder, whatever—enough to unbalance him and make him think better of trapping me here. A quick glance down confirms it—this is one of the tallest trees on the steep slope. Neither of us can fall here and hope to survive. Many, many fire-voices travel on the night air, but they are drowned out by the whooshing in my ears.

And the impact comes. My feet smash into him all right, but he only makes a small noise of discomfort and I realise: I have judged this badly. Very, very badly.

Because the man in the prisoner's clothes has held on to my boot. And I find myself dangling in mid-air between my branch and his vice-like grip. 'Let go!' I grunt between snatched breaths.

He shakes his head. It must cost him some effort to hold on to me and keep himself steady against the trunk. But he has a chance.

I do not. Already, I feel my hands lose grip. Is he really

such a villainous murderer that he would throw a child off a high tree with no regret? 'Let go...' I groan again. 'Please, sir'.

He holds on. 'Come down here, boy! Before it's too late.'

There would be no 'too late' if he hadn't climbed my tree. But I have no choice. With the last of my strength, I move my hands along the branch back to the trunk. He doesn't let go of my boot, but he gives me a little room for manoeuvre. With a final effort, I slide down the trunk towards the stranger. Coming to sit on a thick branch a little above his head, I sigh deeply and shake out my hands and arms. I hadn't noticed the pain till now. Down there in Castle Street, servants and masters still stare at the giant flames pouring up into the sky from the market. They don't know I'm trapped by a criminal and about to die. I feel the fight go out of me.

The prisoner below me is bearded and his stripy grey suit glares against the dimness all around. It must be the early hours of the morning now. Even though the town is burning, servants in the street gradually retreat to their houses. Of course; their masters will still want breakfast in the morning.

'Take yer boots off. And yer jerkin. Yer scarf too.'

'But why...' The question sticks in my throat as he makes a quick move towards me. He is still standing on the branch below, but towering over me now, trapping me tight. There's nothing for it but to obey. I unlace my boots and hand them over. He lets them dangle from his hand. Hesitating, I unbutton my jerkin. It's awkward to wriggle out of it, perching on a branch and having a monster of a man breathe down my neck, but I manage it. I try not to think about the fact that, if anyone finds my body after this, it'll be dressed in undergarments.

He accepts my clothes without comment and glances at the emptying street. 'Come, boy!' he mumbles. 'Before the screws come looking fer me.' He has squeezed his bulk into my jerkin and carefully ties the prisoner's shirt into a thick, prickly part of the tree. 'They'll be looking fer the clothes. But they'll no' look up. Might buy us some time.'

I shiver, but I don't shift.

'Listen, I willnae harm ye. But they'll be looking fer a man on his own, no' a man and a boy. I'll let ye go once I'm clear o' them.' His eyes dart up the hill and along the river, ahead and behind.

'NOW, boy! Come. And wheesht!' His whisper is gruff and urgent.

The night air sizzles with sparks and shouts, over in the town. The man indicates the opposite direction: the river, and further down, the islands. Darkness hangs thick over there. I feel my face contort into a grimace: only a few hours ago, my worst worry was a beating from my guardian. Now I'm at the mercy of an escaped prisoner, and I don't know what else to do, other than obey.

Once out of view of the prison, we drop to the ground and he wriggles my boots onto his bare feet, taking a lace and looping my wrist to his.

They're my father's boots, I want to shout. *It's all I have left.*

We head down the steep slope, dodging the light and keeping to bushes and shadows. The water laps gently and we move south, away from the town where countless pails are sure to be passed in the futile fight against the flames. I turn my back on Inverness, on Uncle Ewan, on my past. I turn my back on the light, cast by a million dancing flames in the sky.

And I follow the stranger into the darkness.

CHAPTER 4

The Travellers

He walks ahead, around the back of the last few houses on the edge of Inverness, where the trees are dense. The sky is so filled with smoke that even if there was moonlight, it would make no difference. Suddenly he motions for me to stop and cranes his neck.

'Wait here, boy. Dinnae move.' And he crouches low and approaches one of the houses from the back, ducking as he gently pushes the gate. It opens, and he disappears into the yard. Moments later, he reappears, wearing a man's shirt and breeches. He almost smiles for the first time. 'Left their washing out overnight, didn't they? Bit loose…' He makes a face. 'And damp! But good enough.'

I catch my jerkin and jacket, but putting it on again is hard, with my hands and limbs so clammy and stiff. The man stares at the house for a long time, taking it in— whitewashed and low. Not a rich person's home.

He shakes himself out of his reverie. 'Time!' he says. 'We don't have long.' As if they had heard him over in the town, the bells begin to ring at the Sherriff Court, competing with the fire bell that has been sounding for an hour? Two? I simply don't know anymore.

It seems that we walk, stumble or run all night. The horizon in the east starts to lighten, and my eyes are heavy with grief and tiredness when I sink down.

'I can't...' I begin, and the man nods. Thankfully, the woods are thick here. He pulls me up one last time. 'Away from the river, boy. They might use boats tae look for me.'

With no blanket or pillow, I'm not sure it is sleep, but I sink into an exhausted stupor in seconds. Beside me the man keeps watch with narrow eyes, leaning against a tree. Nothing matters anymore, I decide, and allow myself to drift into a world where I had a mother, a father and a sister, and where fires and sausages and ruffians do not exist.

When I wake, the smoke is less stinging in the air. The man lies sleeping, I think; his head resting on a mossy patch. He looks almost peaceful, like he couldn't do harm to a single soul. But that's not likely, given the fact he is a prisoner. Was.

I swallow hard.

I am the prisoner now.

It's as if he can sense my gaze on his face. His nose wrinkles, he blinks and with a start, scrambles to an upright position.

Like me, he needs a moment to adjust to this new reality, which gives me a chance to look at him properly. Tall he is, even taller than Uncle Ewan, and that's saying something. His beard is unkempt, as you'd expect of a prisoner, and he is thin, but muscles ripple beneath the stolen shirt sleeves. Make no mistake—he'll be strong, that one. Flecks of grey glisten in his hair, but not many. Most of it is the colour of dirty sand. His eyes flit around like trapped mice—no trace of tiredness in them now.

'Slept alright?' he mutters and then shrugs. 'Ye learn not to sleep too deeply in prison.'

And there, he has said it. The criminal. I stare at my feet and rub my backside where dampness has seeped in.

The sun is high. How late is it?

Again, the man seems to have read my mind. 'Afternoon,' he says. 'We'll need tae push on soon.' I don't have to ask why—he needs to put as much distance between himself and the prison as possible. But I need to go home. Don't I? I try to imagine dragging myself back through Uncle Ewan's door: the barefoot boy who burnt down the market. A large image of Uncle Ewan's hands fills my mind and I can almost feel the pain.

Don't fool yourself, Phineas. The night guard will blame me, again and again. There is no hope. There is no home anymore.

The man keeps staring at me without looking away.

'Long story?' he asks.

I nod.

'Do ye ever talk?'

I surprise myself by answering. 'Sir, with respect, I don't know you.'

'I could be a villain. Is that what you mean?' The corners of his mouth curl up. He laughs quietly and I think hard about running. *There is no knowing what this man will do to me.*

Oh Lord, did I just say that aloud?

'Listen tae me properly, right? I dinnae hurt kids. I'll let you go unharmed, never fear. But for now, I need ye. The Sheriff officers have already been along the road twice while ye were sleeping. They are looking for an escaped prisoner. Though, tae be fair, the guards left the key in the lock of my cell themselves, when they hurried off tae help the fire brigaders. The point is, they'll no' be looking for a poor man in ordinary attire travelling along the road with his son. And once we're clear, I'll let you go. But don't breathe a word, all right?'

I shake my head.

'And my name is Mr Robertson. John Robertson. In case ye wanted tae know.'

There is a pause.

'I'm Phineas.' I finally say.

He nods and stoops to gather our things before he

21

realises that there is nothing to gather.

'I say we follow the road, but stay up here, under the cover.'

'Yes, Mr Robertson, sir,' I answer and the man looks at me as if I'd said something funny. He stretches his hands towards me and I flinch back instinctively. Too many hands have flown at me in rage; I simply can't help myself. And the man looks at me again, long and thoughtful.

'Helping ye up, that's all,' he mutters, but takes a step back and I mumble an apology.

It's difficult work to negotiate the fallen branches and the roots and the loose ground. More than once we disturb a fox, or a nest of birds, or a deer. Food now consumes my mind—the last time I ate was last night. I curse myself for delivering the parcel. My mouth salivates just thinking about sausages. I keep my eyes open for berries, but raspberries and hazelnuts don't seem to grow where I am looking. The brambles are nowhere near ripe yet.

'Best tae stay on this side of the loch. We'll get to the monastery at Fort Augustus. They'll feed us. One more night.'

I wince with every step. There's a thorn in my left foot, but I can't get it out and the pain is getting worse. When I know he's not looking, I glare at the boot-thief walking ahead. It achieves nothing, of course, but it does make me feel a great deal better.

By then, our evening shadows stretch long on the ground. I can't help imagining Uncle Ewan's rage, with his livelihood gone. The more I imagine, the more certain I become that I can never go back.

After a couple of hours, we see a column of smoke ahead and Mr Robertson slows down. 'A camp. Careful now; let's walk on the road. They might be suspicious otherwise.'

To my surprise, he makes straight for it, slow and steady. We hear laughter in the distance: a young girl, perhaps, and at least two voices besides.

My foot is throbbing so badly by now that I can barely put weight on it. Mr Robertson sighs and stoops low. 'Climb on my back. We'll never get anywhere otherwise.'

Even with a loaded pistol held to my head, I would not step near such a man of depravity by choice, but I haven't been more desperate in my life. I allow him to carry me.

And we round a bend where a flickering fire lights up the roadside and where the last sunrays glint on the surface of a beautiful painted caravan. The words '*Professor Moffat's Entertainment*' are written in swirling letters on the side.

A girl is dancing without music a little way off, pirouetting, falling to the ground, pirouetting again, falling, pirouetting for a last time, staying upright and whooping in triumph. Her hair is dark, but her skin pale, bathed in orange and golden light. The water washes up gently on the shore.

By the fire, a man with a dark door-knocker beard and a showman's smile picks at a fiddle, the bow lying by his feet. A woman with a patched skirt carries out a hunk of bread to him. Some way off, a Clydesdale horse grazes in the clearing. The man jumps up with surprising agility as we approach.

'Evening,' Mr Robertson says, 'How are you all this evening?' It's a polite Highland greeting. More polite than these people are used to, perhaps.

'Good evening,' the showman answers and looks us up and down.

'I wonder if I could trouble you for a favour,' Mr Robertson says. 'My, erm, son here has hurt his foot. He lost his own boots and had tae go barefoot, and he's struggling now. We were hoping to reach the Fort, but...'

Step by step they approach us, the entertainer, his wife, the girl. The man whispers something in the woman's ear, and she steps forward and shakes hands. 'Let's see if I can help. I know a bit about herbs and Ishie here has had her fair share of splinters from dancing on that old stage. Would you like a bite to eat? We haven't got very much but...'

'My boy is hungry, I thank you. May God reward you.'

His voice is still gruff. He drops me down by the fire, and I wince loudly as the pain of the impact shoots up my body.

The woman isn't fazed. 'It's swollen, it is. Ishie, get me the bag. You know the one. Merriweather, see to the pot a minute, will you?'

Her husband nods and walks over to the fire.

The dancing girl emerges from the caravan with a worn leather purse. In her other hand, she offers a chunk of bread which I devour without thinking of my manners at all. Mr Robertson holds my foot up high towards to fire. The woman takes one look and before I know it, a sharp pain consumes me. She has made a cut to release the thorn. Blood and pus ooze out and the tension gives way.

'Hold still now,' she urges as she rubs a green tincture from a glass bottle over the cracks. It stings, but in a good way. The girl called Ishie wraps the area in a bandage. I wriggle my toes.

'We're much obliged, good lady,' says Mr Robertson and I add "thank you" before he continues: 'It was kind of you to help. But we'd best be off. We may yet get a little further before we make our camp.'

The woman looks shocked. 'But what about that fugitive? Haven't you heard? It's not safe out there. Not when there's a violent villain on the loose. They say he was awaiting trial for attempted murder, he was. And he escaped.'

CHAPTER 5

PHIN

Attempted murder.

The words land like a thump in my stomach. Mr Robertson composes himself very quickly.

'Ah, dinnae believe all the stories you hear, good lady!' His mouth begins a smile, but his eyes are not joining in.

The girl runs over. 'They aren't stories, sir. Two officers from the Inverness Castle have come past today already. There's all sorts of trouble in Inverness these days. There was a big fire in the town, they say, and all the warders from the castle were needed to help fight the flames. They say he must have picked the lock of his cell. What a villain, to take such shameless advantage. Now they are looking for him everywhere.'

'That's enough talking, Ishie,' her father calls from the fireside.

She rolls her eyes behind her father's back and dances across the clearing. The showman's face bears no trace of a smile anymore. Joining us, he adds: 'But my daughter's right in one thing: it may not be wise to travel on, even if you don't have anything valuable. That man would probably steal the very clothes off your back if he had the chance, and send your soul to heaven while he's at it.'

Robertson looks alarmed. He knows it: I could unmask him, this very moment.

A million thoughts crash through my mind.

Could four of us overwhelm him? Robertson would surely win any struggle and dispatch us all, if he's a man willing to kill. Uncle Ewan flashes briefly through my mind, an early memory so terrible I can't even think the thought through to its end. And to the world, I'm a fire-raiser—half of me believes it myself.

No, I can't risk betraying this man who will stop at nothing.

And of course, a travelling showman can't be trusted either; Uncle Ewan has often talked about their kind. Their frivolous storytelling and their wild music, and their unrespectable ways in all things, Punch's Opera and conjuring and acrobatics.

Mr Robertson's eyes beg mine. He carried me. I remember his outstretched hand to help me up. He gave the bread to me and didn't have any himself.

And the moment passes.

The showman's fancy beard twitches into a smile. 'Why don't you two share our fire tonight? Tomorrow you can get a lift on the cart to Fort Augustus and go your own way. You see, if that criminal got hold of you, or your son, your blood would be on my conscience.'

Robertson hesitates.

Is he going to make me hobble out into the cold again?

He is not.

'That would be terribly kind of ye; we're very much in yer debt.'

The entertainer grins and bows, stretching out his hand. 'Merriweather Moffat.' He indicates: 'My wife, Alice. And Ishbel, of course.'

'Ishie,' she corrects.

'John Robertson. And this is Phineas. Allow me.'

He disappears into a nearby copse and drags a thick trunk over to the fire to serve as a bench. Ishie stands aside to make room, open-mouthed. 'Did you see that Mother?' Meaningful glances pass between them all, but I am too tired and too sore to care.

We share a thin soup, though there is meat in it, and potatoes. Mr Robertson is quiet but pleasant, asking questions and listening as our hosts talk at length, about the places where they have performed. How they passed through Inverness the day before the fire. 'Better that we're gone. It's always the travelling folk who get the blame for such things. Regrettable.' The showman shakes his head.

For a moment, I'm so impressed that I forget that I am

on the run. 'You've been to the Rosehaugh House? The big one across the water?'

'For a house party last week, yes,' Ishie laughs. 'We perform, you see. It's what we do. Father does a puppet play for children, in posh houses or in the streets.' She flicks her dark hair over her shoulder.

'My father has a bad back, so the lifting is hard. But we're managing. I'm pretty strong.'

I look at her more closely, and I believe her.

'What about you? What's your name again?' She looks at me, really looks at me.

'Phineas,' I say and promptly start spluttering. Something unspecified from the broth has got stuck in my throat. Without hesitation, Ishie whacks me on the back, hard. 'Is it gone?'

I want to protest, but there is no denying it: her method worked.

'See? Done it before,' she says, chewing and grinning with her mouth open and I almost turn around, waiting for Miss Garrow to sneer in her high, disapproving voice. Waiting for Uncle Ewan's voice to land on me like a whip, before his hand fell, as it inevitably would. Behaving properly was more important than religion in Uncle Ewan's house. Which is why my sister Lizzie was never talked about at all.

'What's up with you?' she asks, mouth hanging open, a half-grin still there from a moment ago.

'It's… I lived in my, erm, uncle's house for a while, and he was terribly keen on… being proper. He would have given me a beating for what you did there.'

She looks genuinely puzzled and turns around as if wondering whether anyone else has seen her doing anything improper, because she certainly remembers nothing of the sort.

'You chewed with your mouth open. And spoke at the same time.'

'Your uncle sounds like an ogre!' She grins again. 'Just as well your father isn't like him! Bit quiet though, isn't he?'

I nod, wondering how I am going to extricate myself from this right old mess.

'Oh, and I don't think I like the name Phineas,' Ishie announces. 'I'm going to call you Phin instead. No point arguing. Ishie has spoken!'

Phin.

The new me.

Phineas was the well-mannered butcher's delivery boy whose parents died and whose sister no one talked about. The one who was in the wrong place at the wrong time. The one who set the market on fire.

Phin? He is someone different altogether. He is the coward runaway who took flight, rather than try to clear his name. The one who keeps company with criminals and travelling girls with messy hair and bad manners and loud laughs. The one who has no boots and no idea what in the world to do next.

The girl gets up and crawls into the caravan as I stoke the fire and build it up for the night. Wrapped in borrowed coats, we lie down beside it, but all the while I see another fire, many miles north from here.

The night is star-speckled, away from the gas-lights of the streets. The owls hoot in the woods and Mr Robertson, if that's even his real name, is twitching. He is bound to be troubled.

But not half as frightened as me. If the stories are true, the man across the campfire from me is a violent evildoer. And I am his hostage.

I need to get away. But where to? Like it or not, Mr Robertson is the only company I can keep now.

I pretend to sleep. The fire beside us burns low, and there has long been silence in the caravan, when I shiver with the cold and become aware: the convict has shifted and silently got to his feet. I shut my eyes tightly as he drops more sticks onto the fire to keep it going, but then his footsteps approach, cracking twigs and crunching needles under each step. I can sense him, leaning over me, and hesitating. Is he unsure whether to go through with something? I confess all my misdeeds in a split-second prayer, for fear that my last hour has come.

CHAPTER 6

KINDNESS FROM UNEXPECTED PLACES

I feel a weight on my shoulder. Not a hand, but something soft and heavy. I'm so surprised that I do open my eyes, and he's put his coat over me. All he is wearing now is the flimsy shirt from the washing line. He catches my eye in the firelight and sinks back into his space across from me, wrapping his arms around himself and curling up as close to the fire as he can without singeing the hairs on his arms. I whisper my thanks into the night air. No-one has ever done anything so selfless for me.

I imagine the hands which so gently placed the coat around me, trying to throttle the life out of another, and shudder. *Can someone be a kind man and a murderer?*

I wake the next morning as Ishie stumbles past, a cloth wrapped around her dripping hair. 'The loch is right there. I might as well make myself respectable!' she laughs. She shakes her hair one more time, right above me, and I squeal a little. Mr Robertson chuckles, but his eyes dart to the road. And I hear what he hears. Hoof beats, two horses. I can tell how many by the sound, although it is not as clear as cobbles. He holds my gaze as two sheriff officers trot past, notice us and stop. Ishie and her father emerge from the caravan.

'Can I help you, good sir?' offers the showman, but he is completely ignored.

'Travellers!' snaps one of the officers. 'Couldn't trust them as far as you could throw them. Probably in league with all the criminals in the country.'

I can't believe the officer would talk like this. Those to whom he is referring are right here, listening. But they don't react to the provocation.

'Listen to me, you lot. We're after an escaped prisoner. A dangerous man, travelling alone. He should not be approached; extremely vicious he is. We have reason to believe he might have come this way.'

'No one like that has come this way, officers,' says Alice Moffat. 'Have you seen anything?' She directs that last sentence straight to Mr Robertson who has stood in the shadows of the caravan.

He moves stiffly, and his face is stretched. His voice sounds high when he answers. 'Me? No, I… erm… we never noticed anything. Never seen anyone, eh?' I shake my head, too. Mr Robertson busies himself with the washing line, undoing the knots and packing everything up. The officers shrug at each other.

'Maybe he went north after all,' the first comments to his colleague before turning back to us.

'Well, if you see a tall man, strong and rough, don't approach him. You've a duty to report it if you do. Have you lot heard the news of the fire?'

There is a funny moment where I have the urge to laugh, out of sheer panic and embarrassment.

Thankfully, the officer continues without noticing: 'They say a butcher's boy sneaked back into the market, seemingly deranged. The only witness is the night porter. Tried his best to stop the boy, bless him, but the rascal smashed in the gas pipes and set the market on fire. The whole building burnt to the ground, would you believe! Sad case, orphan and all. Gone on the run of course, so we're keeping our eyes open, but he'd never have got as far as this. No matter.'

The showman's wife leans forward and opens her mouth, but seems to think better of it and closes it again.

'And here is the likeness of the prisoner, in case you do see something. Your kind often do.'

'We will be vigilant,' Professor Moffat says and steps forward to take the leaflet, offering to shake hands. But the officer wrinkles his nose and reins his horse sidewards. He throws the paper to the ground, nods to his companion and trots back onto the road, towards Fort Augustus. We hear him shout as they ride off. 'If the ruffian is going to seek shelter anywhere, it'll be at the Abbey.'

The officers' horses' hoofbeats are swallowed up by the road, the water laps up and down the shore, gentle and sure. But I can barely breathe. Ishie looks at me with narrow eyes, her father folds out the leaflet, nods as if it merely confirmed his worst fears, and holds it up for all to see.

It's not a great likeness of my travelling companion, but beneath, it says in great, clear letters, so even I can read it easily: John Robertson. Awaiting trial for attempted murder. Do not approach.

Mr Robertson's head sinks and I can feel my muscles tense.

Trapped animals are most dangerous of all; everyone knows that. *What will he do?*

CHAPTER 7

An Honest Man

'I'm no murderer,' he says, in a very small voice for someone so tall. 'I'm no' a violent man.'

'And I'm no fire-raiser.' It's out of my mouth before I even think it. 'I'm not.'

Merriweather Moffat and his wife look at each other, terror and confusion and indecision in their features, all at the same time. Ishie steps forward but is held back by her mother. 'You're not father and son?'

I shake my head, relieved. No more lies. Uncle Ewan used to say that secrets and lies are close bedfellows. Miss Garrow sometimes shook her head at him behind his back when he spoke so. Before that, the business with Elizabeth was a hallowed secret in my parents' house: my sister's downfall, never spoken of for the honour of our family. I hated that secret, too.

'I couldnae kill another in God's image.' Robertson's voice is weak. It's waiting for a verdict.

Again, Ishie speaks first. 'Mother, I wonder if Mr

Robertson here is good with his hands? Just while Father's back is bad? And I wonder if Phin here could turn his hand to the puppetry, like Father wanted? An extra pair of hands?'

What's she saying?

'Why did you tell us your real name?' Merriweather Moffat carefully approaches the criminal, who is crouching on the ground beside the caravan.

Robertson looks up, some fire returning to his voice. 'Because I am no liar. Because I am an honest and honourable man, whatever anyone may say.'

I think of the desperation with which he trapped me on the tree.

But also of the kindness as he covered me with his only coat.

'And they think *you* set the Inverness market on fire!' Ishie shakes her dark mane out, still damp from earlier.

'Mr Robertson,' begins Ishie's father, hesitant at first, but surer with every word, looking to his wife for confirmation. 'I think it best if we call you by a middle name for now. Do you have one?'

Robertson looks up, surprised. 'Fergus.'

'Why don't you finish packing up, Fergus. And I think you two should stay in the caravan when we pass the Fort. I take it you won't go to the Abbey now?'

Mr Robertson speaks haltingly, barely believing. 'Why

are ye doing this, sir? Why are you helping me?'

'Because I trust my instinct. I knew you were a good sort when you let the boy eat and didn't take anything for yourself last night. When you lent us a hand, and when you spoke to us with respect. And it's true that we could do with a strong man around—my back is failing and I'm relying on Ishie to do more than a girl of her age should.'

'I can do it all, too,' Ishie interjects before she realises she is undermining her own argument.

'We haven't got much, but if you like, you may share the journey with us for a while and we'll see how we get along. You help us; we help you. If we choose to part company, we do it in a calm and proper way, and that is all there is to it. Phineas, go and help Ishie get some firewood and bundle it up before we leave. Looks like we'll be travelling through Fort Augustus instead of stopping.'

I've prayed for this, but I didn't have faith it could happen, really. That I should escape without hurting a soul, that I should find shelter without deception. Mr Robertson's eyes well up, but Mrs Moffat brushes him off. 'Now, none of that, before we change our minds.'

Hurriedly, he goes to take the washing line down and Ishie nudges me to come with her. We collect twigs in silence, break longer branches to lengths and tie them together with twisted reed from the riverside. It's quiet, deliberate work, and I watch her closely. Her knots hold the first time while my bundles disintegrate and rain to the ground, but I soon get the hang of it.

'Don't make them too big, or too tight, Phin—that way you can throw the whole thing on the fire.' She shows me.

I nod and obey, wondering how old she is. It's so hard to tell, without a bonnet or an apron, with her patched skirt. She looks younger than she is, I'm sure, with her hair in such a loose knot, and without anything being done in the proper way.

'Quit your mumbling! I'm *thirteen*,' she announces.

Did I do it again? 'Sorry.'

'No need. So, are you going to tell me what really happened at the market or not?'

I begin hesitantly, but soon I am in full flow. I leave nothing out, and it feels so good that I want to cry. She is properly outraged at the night porter. 'That man deserves to be imprisoned himself!'

'It was an accident. He fell, that's all.'

'But he gave you all the blame, and you only a boy! Unforgivable!'

It's lovely and new: that someone should take my side. Whenever I got a beating from the schoolmaster, Miss Garrow would say: 'Pain builds the character, makes us obedient and aware of our sinfulness.'

We return to the camp with armfuls of firewood and Merriweather Moffat nods approvingly. 'Now, get in and we'll try our luck.'

I'm glad of the words. "We" and "our".

It's a miracle how much fits into this caravan. High beneath the roof runs a rail of puppets: glove puppets and marionettes, each on its own hook, and a few strung across like a washing line. Painted planks, which I imagine assemble into a booth, are stacked against the side of the wagon, held up by a carved and painted chest. A fiddle hangs from a nail on one side, a simply made harp on the other, and a small paraffin light dangles in between. Beneath the puppets is a row of pots and pans. A neat pile of blankets sits on the floor, patch-worked, yes, but embroidered too. A bucket with beautiful carved roses made from wooden twigs rattles in the corner and I stare in wonder.

'Tuck yourself in there.' Ishie's mother leans in and points to a low table. Beneath it, there is barely enough room for a skinny twelve-year old. Mr Robertson can't hide; he simply has to hope for the best.

Alice Moffat smiles. 'We won't rush through. They expect us to sell and to perform, and we'll do it.'

With this she pulls the curtain and we are instantly bathed in the dull, warm light shining through the patterned fabric.

I don't know what to say, so I don't say anything at all. He whispers though. 'I'm truly sorry for getting you into trouble, boy.'

'I was in plenty trouble already,' I whisper back and we both grimace.

Before long we can hear crowds gathering. The showman reaches in and unhooks the fiddle without even looking, and his wife takes the reins as he strikes up the starting chord. I can hear the crowds clap and risk lifting the heavy fabric a little and peeking out. Ishie dances and walks on her hands and does back flips. She is wild and free and happy, smiling to the crowd and bowing and skipping right up to some of the gentlemen in the crowd and twirling with them before dancing ahead of the wagon once more. It's hard to believe that she is the same species as Miss Garrow. Was Elizabeth wild like this? Was that why she ran and never came back?

Ishie twirls and twirls, and I count the spins: five, six, seven... is she going to fall? No, she lunges forward into a forward roll and has so much momentum that she does another straight after. Beneath her dress, she wears a funny sort of garment, allowing her the freedom and preserving her modesty, I imagine. The fiddle stops. Ishie pulls a bonnet from her sleeve, and just as people try to turn away and avoid paying, she skips up to them again, panting from the effort and smiling with reddened cheeks. No wonder the coins jingle into the white fabric and she catches her father's smile. He leans backwards into the caravan again, hangs the fiddle back onto its hook, slides the bow under the strings, and feels around for the bucket of wooden roses.

'Buy a beautiful bloom for your lady, sir.'

It's Ishie again, walking ahead gracefully and presenting the roses to the crowd one by one. 'Only tuppence a bloom, she'll love you more if you buy her threescore.'

Her voice rings out loud and clear. I could never be so forward!

We come to a halt in the square and both of us duck down deep as the travellers trade—and gossip.

Some people ask news of Inverness. *Did you see the market burn? Is it true that a devil boy conjured up fire with his bare hands and disappeared in a puff of smoke? Is it true that a hundred prisoners ran in all directions as the officers fought the flames?*

Ishie stays quiet at this point and lets her father talk, and Professor Moffat has exactly the sort of voice which should tell a story. All listen; young and old, and more coins tinkle into the copper pan he holds out for his services. I know he never saw any of it, but he describes the night sky lit by burnt gold, as the flames forced the solid sandstone walls to the ground, nowt but a smouldering pile of ashes now. He describes the market traders, appearing one by one, and paints their anguish as they see their livelihoods destroyed. He invents an old woman who ignored all warnings and ran in, only to be forced back by the unbearable heat, her hair singed.

More coins clang into the pot; people are hungry for more.

An hour or two later, I feel stiff and sore, but we must lie still. Mr Robertson has his eyes closed, but I know he isn't sleeping.

'And now, ladies and gentlemen we must move on. We are a day behind as it is.'

'How can you be a day behind?' a voice asks.

'We are travelling right across the country. You can be sure that we'll have better and wilder stories to tell next time.'

'But I need my pot fixed,' some woman calls out.

'Be patient, good lady. We will return. Until then, goodbye.'

The pot-woman answers, irritated: 'You won't go anywhere in a hurry. The sheriff officers have blocked the road ahead, they're searching every cart and carriage.'

In the caravan, Mr Robertson's eyes have pinged wide, wide open.

CHAPTER 8

THE BONNET AND THE BLANKET

We stare at each other, motionless as Alice Moffat cracks her whip and the caravan jerks forward.

Silently, we cast about for better hiding places. Every nook is full of wares; there is simply no room. The is no other exit either, the canvas is tied down properly at the back to stop curious children peering in. *How long do we have, how long?* I can't bear causing this remarkable family any trouble, when they have taken such risks for us. Desperately, I finger through the chest. Clothes. I throw something over to Mr Robertson and reach in again. I have no time to think—pulling on a dress over my rolled-up breeches, and a bonnet, too with a shawl over it all to hide the fact I have no hair; not like a girl does anyway. My voice hasn't broken yet, but I'll have to make it as high as I can if I'm summoned to speak. The cart is already slowing when I finish my work and turn around. Mr Robertson's considerable bulk simply refuses to fit into the traveller woman's dress. I yank at it, but it will not close. 'Blanket!' I hiss as quietly as I can, and reach down to throw the patchwork over him. 'Keep it close to your head. Lie down, face the wall. Stay still.'

My panicked commands are obeyed without question. Mr Robertson's fear twitches in every line of his face. Of course; if one such as he is captured again, the noose awaits. Running away only proves his guilt; it's what Uncle Ewan would say. And until a day or two ago, I might have believed the same.

The wheels creak.

'Halt! No one may pass without being searched.'

Tension floods my brain. The voice doesn't sound like either one of the two officers who came by the camp yesterday, but I can't be certain.

'Surely you won't want to search through all this mess in there. You know how we lot live.' You have to admire Professor Moffat for trying.

'Orders, I'm afraid.'

'But Officer, really.' The showman makes a good job of sounding relaxed. He is a puppeteer, isn't he? An actor. 'Officer, I must protest. There is no-one in here…'

The curtain is pulled back roughly and a uniformed man clambers in—followed by Merriweather Moffat who doesn't miss a beat.

'Apart from my old sister, bless her. She has been afflicted by a terrifying condition, I wouldn't get too near if I was you. My niece is with her, but it's a miserable existence sir. I thank you for not disturbing them in their discomfort. My niece has been suffering. We fear it may be contagious to the point of death.'

'I'm feeling right sick, sir,' I splutter, high-pitched. My voice is weak with panic, so I don't even have to pretend much. I flutter my lashes as I think a caring girl might.

The officer clambers back a safe distance and nearly falls over the pile of blankets.

'The ailing woman. Can I question her?'

I drop my volume to a high whisper. 'Sir, she does nothing but lie with her face to the wall, all day long.'

The showman interrupts loudly. 'Ah, no! I can smell something. Go check her bedclothes and see if she has soiled herself again!'

The speed with which the sheriff officer retreats is remarkable.

'Nothing to worry about in here,' he shouts to his colleague outside. He struggles out, looking over his shoulder as I protectively pull the blanket over Mr Robertson's shoulders.

The caravan jiggles into motion again. We are too terrified to move until the showman's wife puts her head through the curtain. Ishie's head appears above hers. Both wear broad grins. 'We only wanted to see it!' Ishie chuckles, and the woman giggles, which is a very unladylike thing to do. Her daughter, meanwhile, has controlled her voice: 'We're leaving the Fort behind now. We'd better give you some privacy. You're lucky I'm no good at drawing, otherwise I'd make you sit for a portrait and draw your likeness. I may try anyway…'

I lean forward and pull the curtain shut in front of her face. 'Give us a moment, please!'

The two female voices chortle loudly behind the fabric.

It takes a good deal of wriggling on both our parts to free ourselves of the loathsome costumes, but when I say so, Mr Robertson looks at me seriously. 'They are the best this woman has, and we shouldnae ridicule them. There's many folk have nae more than the clothes on their backs.'

He looks thoughtfully into the distance then, and I wonder if he is thinking back to that cottage by the River Ness where he stole his attire off the line. Was the person in that cottage such a poor soul?

Still staring, Mr Robertson says it like a vow: 'I'll pay them all back. All who help us, I will pay them back for the favour they have shown.'

We are well along Loch Lochy by the time we stop for the evening. The sun is setting over the hills on the opposite side and Mr Robertson has staked a few fishing lines. Ishie and I dig for bait and find all sorts of worms. A line begins to twitch and slowly, very slowly, Mr Robertson hauls it in. He's fashioned the hook himself, and a good one it is too—it doesn't give way, even though the fish on the other end is enormous.

I build and light the fire. Soon the fish turns on a spit above it, its skin charring as the fresh aroma is released. The pebbles move gently in and out with the water, the evening sky turns pink and I feel that heaven cannot be so very far away. I eat more than my fill as Mrs Alice Moffat cooks flat scones on a griddle. Bread, butter and fresh fish! What in the world does the Queen herself eat that could be better than this?

Ishie giggles every few minutes or so, waving the bonnet I wore and daring me to put it on again, until I give her a playful skelp with a cloth and she leaves me be.

The next day we travel through the most magnificent scenery on this earth. Mr Robertson and I don't hide now, but take it in turns between us to hitch a ride on the back of the caravan and to lead the Clydesdale. I was wary of the beast at first, on account of its size, but it's beautiful really, and a friendly creature, if a bit stubborn. Its ribs are showing, and I'm glad of the thick grass it can feast on every time we make camp.

It's not as if I really need to know, but I am curious. 'Where are we going, Ishie?'

She chews on a long blade of grass and whistles through the gap in her teeth. 'Not sure. Father won't say. I overheard Mother saying something about Perth last night. But Perth is not so very special, we've been there before.' She wrinkles her forehead.

I check the six traps we have put out, and one has got a rabbit, which is all we need, or so Ishie says. She tucks her thick dark hair right into her collar and sets to work, skinning the animal. I help and am glad of something to do that I'm actually good at.

'I didn't expect you to know how to skin a rabbit,' she says, a shred of respect creeping into her voice.

'My guardian is a butcher. I help with the meat sometimes, but most of the time I run around the town and deliver all the orders. Well, I did deliver the orders. Hogmanay is my favourite day of the year. After all the extra trade, Uncle Ewan is in a good mood, and there is no work to be done at all; we have a proper New Year feast with the neighbours.'

'What are the neighbours like? I've never had any.'

That makes complete sense when you think about it, but I'm still taken aback. 'Well, some are friendly enough. But Ishie, didn't you ever go to school?'

'No,' she answers cheerfully.

'But I thought you were obliged? Isn't there a law or something, to say everybody must?'

Her eyes blaze. 'I know enough to get by! All I need to know is how to dance and sell things. Who needs school for that? And my Mother has taught me the harp and lots and lots of stories, and I can cook and hunt and...'

'Very well! I didn't mean it like that. I only wondered, that's all.'

The rabbit, jointed, is tucked into the pot with a swig of water from the stream. Ishie carries a belt with small bags sewn on and pulls a pinch of seasoning out.

'That will do,' she says and pats the belt. 'It's got to last, this.'

And as soon as we have secured the pot above the fire, her father comes over towards us.

'No time like the present, Phin. Let's have your first lesson.'

THE ART OF SCREAMING

I don't know why I'm so nervous. We're away from the loch now, and the sheriff officers are not likely to come this far, are they? The showman has chosen a flat bit of ground by the wayside. A stream glistens and tinkles beside us as we assemble the booth, which he calls a fit-up. I struggle a bit, and he huffs and puffs, but Mr Robertson joins us and lifts each piece of wood with one hand, sliding the joints into one another easily. Merriweather Moffat looks genuinely impressed. 'You do have some strength in your arms!'

Robertson merely shrugs, but he does smile and wink as he walks past.

Uncle Ewan could smile, but he never winked. Never. Winking is a 'we're in this together' thing to do.

The fit-up booth is assembled and stands tall now: a three-sided frame of wood, with a window in the widest, middle section and strong fabric stretched over.

'Bit of that paint needs touching up again,' the showman mumbles. 'But it'll have to be neat.'

'I can try that,' volunteers Robertson. 'I did a bit of painting in my time.'

Professor Moffat looks him up and down. 'It matters, you know. People notice. They'll only give us the time of the day if we take pride and do things properly.'

'I understand. I was simply...'

Moffat gesticulates. 'Oh, very well. Try the corner at the bottom there tonight. If it's good, you can do the whole lot. Careful though.'

He turns his attention back to me. 'Ready, young Phineas? You're going to be a great asset to our act. More than two puppets on stage at any one time? Why, it's unheard of! We'll be the talk of every town! Come on now; you're small enough to fit into the space. Have you ever used puppets like this before?' He holds them like they are sacred. He holds them with love, cradling their brightly painted wooden heads like treasure.

I'm in a fairy tale world. The stream sparkles past, the sun is high in the sky and I am simply spellbound. Here they all are! The familiar villain Punch with his hooked nose, his put-upon wife Judy, the Baby, the Policeman, the Hangman. The Devil. I shudder and look over my shoulder, as if Miss Garrow was close by enough to disapprove. But my eyes keep being drawn back to the Policeman. Can a twelve-year-old be hanged for arson?

'Did you even hear me, boy?' The showman takes the

Policeman puppet out of my hand and hands me a dainty-looking wooden girl. 'Here you are. Your voice is still high enough—that'll make it all the easier for me. Go on. Be a puppeteer.'

He disappears to watch, leaving me alone in the booth.

I stare at the puppet in my hand.

Miserably.

'How?'

'Hold her upright. Yes, like that, but not too high so your arm isn't showing. Yes, that's better. And don't let it droop; it's easy to do. Keep her facing out. Right, good. Make her walk left in the window... like that, and then right. Up, down, up, down, like a bobbing motion. Good, that works; now try a faster, smaller movement for running.'

I concentrate hard and sprint my puppet from one end of the stage window to the other. My arms have begun to hurt.

'Not bad, Phin. Now, you need to add a voice. You move the puppet when it's talking, but you keep it still when another puppet is supposed to be speaking, understand? She's on her own now, and she's running and screaming. Show me.'

I can't see him as I'm still crouched inside the booth, but I give it a half-hearted attempt, bobbing my puppet along the window and mumbling... *'aah'*.

'STOP!'

53

I push myself up on my tiptoes and look out through the performance window where Professor Moffat is watching. 'What?' I squirm.

'Boy, that was terrible, that was. I said "scream", not "whisper". We are performing for a big audience, and outside. There will be noisy things going on all around us. You need to reach the child furthest away in the audience, far from you on the other side of the booth. It is an art, make no mistake!'

I take a deep breath. '*Aaaaaargh,*' I try, slightly louder.

'Hmmm. Again, but a hundred times louder, and with your bobbing puppet running left and right, like it doesn't know what to do.'

Not knowing what to do? Now *that* strikes a chord with me. In my mind, I am back in the market, see the flames advancing on the sweets in the stall, the night guard lying helplessly trapped on the floor, the flickering light, the heat and the smoke. I duck back, lift my arms, get my puppet into position and scream, high pitched to imitate a girl's voice, while facing my puppet out, jerking right and left, clutching her head, clasping her hands, running her to the left and the right.

There is silence from the audience side of the booth. I wait for a few seconds and then stretch to lift my head high enough to look out of the window again. My appearance is met with applause, not only from the showman, but Ishie and Mr Robertson, and Alice Moffat, too.

'You'll do grand,' she says. 'With a bit of practice, you'll do just fine.'

CHAPTER 10

ONE OF THOSE MOMENTS

The next days are a blur of travelling and stopping, practising and learning lines. Professor Moffat already has everything memorised, so when I suggest pasting some notes onto the hidden inside of the booth, he simply shakes his head.

I work on my voices. Whiny for the Baby, forceful for Judy, hoarse and angry for the Policeman, while Merriweather Moffat plays Punch with a swazzle, a tiny metal thing which he inserts into the roof of his mouth (how he doesn't choke on it is beyond me). I train my hands and fingers to operate the Dog Toby puppet, my favourite of them all, especially the bit when it steals Mr Punch's sausages. I even manage to wag the tail with my pinkie, and I wish I could both act and watch at the same time.

The Professor tells me story after story and I drink them in—I loved hearing stories at school. But here, I can truly imagine them, hear them in my head, and then simply imitate the voice which that character puppet already has in my imagination. I don't know how, but it seems to work.

We reach the main road between Inverness and Perth at Blair Atholl, and I sense that Mr Robertson is uneasy—maybe because we are seeing sheriff officers passing by from time to time, and the problem of travelling with entertainers is that you are looked at!

'Don't worry, Fergus,' Professor Moffat assures him. 'Hiding in broad daylight is the best kind of hiding. Besides, you're not a bad sort, I know that for certain now. One day you'll tell us your whole story, will you?'

My companion smiles a little tensely, but it's a smile all the same. 'Dinnae hold yer breath, Professor Moffat.'

He has not been idle while I practised puppeteering. Between them, he and Ishie have made up a clowning act; a good idea since the thick paste disguises his face, I suppose. He plays on the Strong-Man notion. Ishie plays tricks on him as he lifts his big logs and drags his heavy stones—and he falls over and lands on his bum and I laugh aloud for the first time I can remember. The more days pass, the more blurry my memories of Inverness get, even though Mr Robertson is a living reminder that it all really happened.

In the evenings, we sit around the fire for a while. Merriweather Moffat has given up trying to teach Ishie the fiddle and gives me a chance. I love the way the instrument lies in my hand. I gently pluck the strings, but it's not long before I hold it between chin and shoulder with confidence. I practise every minute of the day I'm not doing chores or sleeping—puppetry for a while and then back to the fiddle. It takes a few days, but eventually the bow finds the same rhythm as my left hand and I produce a recognisable melody. It's one of those moments: Mr Robertson stretches up above the pile of firewood he was chopping, Ishie freezes in mid-spin and Professor Moffat looks up from the wooden rose he is carving. All look at me.

'Again,' he calls over, leaning forward.

Self-conscious, I arrange the cloth, rest the fiddle on it and concentrate hard. I don't even know what the melody is called, but I bow it for my audience—and they will me on, note by note. It's not perfect—not nearly perfect. But it seems to be impressive enough for Merriweather Moffat to leave his work behind and come closer.

'That's not bad at all, lad.' He rests his hands gently on my shoulder and nods in a silent command. Again, I lift the instrument to my chin, let my fingers remember their place, and raise the bow. This time it is nearly perfect, and he smiles down at me with something that looks like pride.

'Mark my words, Phin—we'll make a performer of you yet.'

CHAPTER 11

NOTHING OUT OF THE ORDINARY

We are approaching Perth, so Ishie was right. But Professor Moffat is still secretive. 'There's something we're picking up in Perth. Something that's going to get us talked about, all over Scotland,' he says.

'Ishie, can you guess his meaning?' I ask her after another conversation ended with Merriweather Moffat tapping his nose and walking away chuckling. She looks infuriated.

'No I can't! But every time we have money to spare, he spends it on something—the Punch and Judy fit-up, for example, and that set of puppets. He was using the marionettes before, but he's always chasing for the next thing, isn't he? The thing that's going to make him big. There are so many entertainers now, you've got to set yourself apart, he says. I only hope he hasn't got himself into any kind of trouble, that's all.'

We reach Perth when it's almost dark, the black river snaking through grand buildings on either side. I have walked for hours and simply want to collapse in a heap by the fire, trying to forget how much this place sounds like Inverness, but Mrs Moffat sends me down to the water. 'I know it's late, Phin, but see if you can catch any fish—you never know. If you haven't any luck quickly, just come back, but you might as well give it a try.'

I sigh and pull my scarf closer around my neck—the nights are chill for July.

As Mr Robertson rigs up the canvas shelter that he and I have slept in for the last few weeks, I stumble down the steep embankment and nearly fall over with fright. There's a figure there, hooded and black against the moonlit water. Quickly, I crouch beside an abandoned cart wheel.

Facing away from me, the man is dragging something behind him. A sack of some sort, almost the size of me. He stands by the water, heaves the weight onto his back and in a swinging, swivelling motion, hurls his load into the river. It doesn't go all the way in, but slowly sinks in the shallows. The man has already turned and strides back towards the town.

A memory stirs. Uncle Ewan, discovering a stray dog and her pups in our shed. He drowned the whole litter in the River Ness before the night was out, despite my begging him not to. How I cried, all night long. And now I know, without a shadow of a doubt, what I am witnessing.

All thoughts of discovery forgotten, I drop the fishing rod and pelt down the embankment and into the shallows.

The shock of the cold and the draw of the water catch me by surprise and almost knock me off my feet, but stretching both arms out sideways like a rope-dancer, I manage to wade forward. My bare feet slide on the slimy pebbles—the greedy river is so much stronger than I thought possible.

All the same, I steadily work my way to the half-submerged sack. By rights it should have floated out of reach already, but it must have snagged on something. I'll get there. I will. The water is up to my knees now, but I push forward, seeing only by dusky moonlight and not taking my eye off the billowing fabric of the sack, for fear of losing sight of it. Two more steps, three maybe. Careful now.

The sack jerks sideways as if to spite me, but I'm close enough to hear a tiny yelp. I was right!

At that very moment, a log with its branches still attached dislodges, nearly sweeps me off my feet, and knocks the sack, which begins to float, slowly but surely, downriver—and out of my reach.

No! I throw myself forward and stretch for it, all thoughts of balance forgotten, getting a little purchase on the material before I crash into the stream and am swept downriver for yards, whether few or many I can't tell. *Breathe, Phineas!* My mind is consumed with two things: *get out* and *don't let go.* The river tears at its prey, both me and the sack, but it's shallow enough for me to claw into the shifting gravel beneath my feet, with toes and with my free hand, inching ever closer to the shore. It doesn't even occur to me to shout for help, deafened as I am by the roar of the water, and the rush of blood in my ears. Finally, it gets shallow enough for me to drop to my knees and I crawl out like an injured beetle, dragging the sack behind me. Dropping flat onto the damp stones of the embankment, I throw myself onto my knees and vomit out river water.

The stars are still there, steady above in the sky. The moon still shines. I still breathe. I am alive, to feel the pain in my cut feet and to shiver with the cold. I am alive.

Again, it feels natural to pray. My mother prayed; my father prayed, and even though Uncle Ewan never did, it's a memory he could not take from me. I thank the Lord for my escape, breathing deeply and allowing myself to feel every passing breeze in my sodden clothes. And then I remember: the sack!

The sack, the sack! It's been lying beside me, so completely still that I hardly dare untie it—and the knot is impossibly tight, especially without much light. No boy my age should have to see what I see now: dead dogs, a little older than the ones Uncle Ewan drowned so many months ago. These ones have hair, sodden and limp.

Too late. It's all I can think as I count: five, six, so small and still. Seven and eight—wait! The seventh pup doesn't feel as cold as the others. I hold it up to the moonlight—a boy. And as I lift the tiny wet body, it gives a hint of a wiggle—I almost miss it, but I know I haven't imagined it. Quickly, I tuck the little creature into my own wet jerkin and double-check the other seven. No, they are completely motionless.

All but one. I managed to save one. Squinting upriver, I see the fishing gear on the embankment. How long have I been gone? I gather my things, along with my strength, and stumble back to camp.

'I was about to come and look fer ye!' says Mr Robertson, not even looking at me and throwing another branch on the fire. 'Nae luck?'

I shake my head. Thankful for the ready shelter, I crawl inside to change into dry clothes—and to examine my new friend without any prying eyes.

I know it's still alive—tiny wriggles against my chest confirm it, but for how long? What do I need to do to *keep* it alive? I carefully extract the dog from my jerkin.

Its fur is softer and drier now, white and grey, with a bit of black around the face, and such a likeness to our Dog Toby puppet. The fire outside casts a ghostly glow and brings on a yawn in boy and dog. I stroke the face of the pup absent-mindedly and it licks my finger. Sucks my finger to tell the truth. I rub its back and start to wonder.

What have I done? There's barely enough food for all of us. What was I thinking? They are going to take it straight down to the river and throw it back in. My heart begins to race again when I think of the grocer's dog in the market. Did it guard the stall until the very end? And the litter of strays in our shed... Again, I look at the tiny wriggling hairy bundle in my hand.

No. Unlike before, this is an animal I might be able to save. Resolutely, I reach for the jug of water Mr Robertson keeps beside his roll-up mattress and dip my finger in, again and again as the little creature licks it off greedily.

'Phin, aren't you coming out? We've some soup and a little bit of bread. Get something to eat before the night's out, surely?' Mrs Moffat's voice is gentle; she almost whispers the words through the canvas. I sigh. I am hungry—ravenous in fact. Reaching for a woollen blanket, I create a loose den for the pup. It makes the tiniest of noises in keeping with its size and its eyes droop. Tucking it in and using my two middle fingers, I give it a final back-rub before heading out to pretend nothing out of the ordinary happened tonight.

During the night, I wake again and again, worrying that I have accidentally rolled on top of my new friend, or that he has died of his weakness. When I finally get to sleep, the pup snuggles gently to my chest under the blanket.

I am roused by the pup's rhythmic licking on my face.

And sense a towering figure standing over me, looking down on me in the dim light of our shelter.

Mr Robertson.

'Explain!' he demands.

Chapter 12

The Mysterious Mission

I tense in anticipation of the blow, before remembering that this is not Uncle Ewan.

Then I scramble upwards, wiping my eyes and nearly dropping the wriggling bundle of fur. The pup winces, which distracts me in my panic so I lose my balance and fall backwards onto the pile of straw. Mr Robertson's bulk begins to shake—he is laughing.

Laughing!

'Explain,' he repeats chuckling and leaning forward—and I flinch back. It's just habit. I'm sure he sees right into my soul at that point. The laughter is wiped from his mouth.

'Come now. Tell me.' There is still some clowning paste in the cracks around his eyes, but he lowers his long body and sits right beside me, holding his hands out to the tiny pup, who wriggles straight into his hands.

I'm on my feet in an instant. 'Give it back, sir!'

I can't let him take it, drown it all over again! I'm about to wrestle the animal off him, or at least I'm about to try, but something stops me: the sight of a huge man like Robertson using his pinkie to stroke the pup gently beneath the chin. The animal closes his eyes and makes a contented rumbling noise.

'I had a wee one like that once. It didnae last long though,' Robertson muses.

'This one will. I'm going to look after it.'

Mr Robertson shakes his head.

'What about Moffat though? Not sure he's gonnae like that.'

'Don't tell them! Please—please don't tell them. I'll keep it quiet. I'll give it food from my own share.' Despite my panic, Mr Robertson is calm, stroking the dog and holding it in the palm of his other hand with ease. His eyes are serious and thoughtful.

'We need these people, Phineas. And they've been good tae us. Dinnae give them a reason to part company.'

I take the puppy back and lower him into the front of my jerkin. 'They don't need to find out. I'm begging you, sir, let me keep it.'

At that very moment, the canvas entrance of our shelter is roughly pulled aside and Mrs Moffat's curly head appears. She lifts her face and reveals a sparkling smile, as if something really exciting was afoot. 'Morning, gentlemen! Keep what?' Will she notice the awkwardness? Mr Robertson stares at his feet like a schoolboy caught cheating and I awkwardly hover my hands over my wriggling clothes.

But Mrs Moffat has already buzzed away without waiting for an answer, humming a tune while Ishie sets out bread and ham for breakfast.

Merriweather Moffat is in excellent form, arranging his puppets on a plank and pointing out their battle wounds of scratches and splinters. 'Ishie and Phin, today is your day— make them well again!'

Like the theatre-man he is, he reveals a box with a rainbow of bottles: the brightest hues—and three brushes, two of them quite thin. 'My wife and I have an appointment in town—and quite an appointment it is! Mr Robertson, would you join us—I wouldn't ask if we didn't need help with this new venture, but we do. You'll see.'

Robertson looks stricken. 'Intae town? Now? Without the clowning disguise?'

'What if he is recognised?' I whisper.

Mrs Moffat throws him a hat from the pile of Moffat hand-me-downs and he pulls it deep into his face.

But nothing can dampen Merriweather Moffat's spirits today. 'No need to look so vexed, my good man. You are one of our party, and that is all there is to it. I'm afraid we simply cannot spare your strength in this endeavour. Isn't that right, my dear?'

Mrs Moffat laughs her tinkly laugh again and I wonder what it must be like for Ishie, having such a mother and father, full of such cheer all the time.

My own ordinary memories of my parents are fading fast. What did Mother's face look like again? Fine-boned like mine, pale, gentle, and a little anxious. My father was devout and serious, principled and stern, but never harsh. And then that last, awful memory which will be forever etched on my mind. Bleeding, rigid and reeking of whisky at the bottom of that stair.

I shake my head to forget, like I ran to forget, too. Now I play fiddle to forget. As soon as the curtain opens, I wriggle my hands for Judy and the Devil and the Policeman and the Dog Toby. To forget. I squeal for the Baby and drop my voice for the Hangman, all the while imagining someone else's head in Punch's noose; someone who truly deserves it.

With all my strength, I resolve to protect the helpless creature tucked into my jerkin.

Because I couldn't protect my father back then.

Ishie nudges me hard. 'Phin! Let's get started, right?'

We spread everything out on a makeshift table, rigged up beside our camp.

'You take Punch—if you make a mess of it, my father can blame you.' She laughs and gets to work on painting over a scratch on the puppet Judy's cheek, no doubt inflicted by Punch's wooden baton. As soon as I look closely, I realise that splinters of wood are missing on my puppet's nose and ears. Ishie sings as we work, and when she runs out of songs,

I sing some hymns I remember. She likes the melodies and soon invents harmonies to sing alongside me. After a while, Ishie is so engrossed in her task that she doesn't seem to notice anything at all, so I sneak to the fire and feed the pup a bit of ham before settling him back into my jerkin where he seems content.

Three or four hours later, the sun is high in the sky and we hear creaking: some sort of wagon wheels. Both of us jump up to see. 'What kind of wagon is that?'

Mr Robertson pulls it along like a horse would. It looks heavy.

The new cart has heavy cloth pulled over it, but it's almost square. Professor Merriweather Moffat and his wife walk behind it like proud parents in a wedding procession. Cheering, Ishie and I race each other to pull back the fabric, but as soon as we get close the adults' faces change.

'Don't touch it!' yells Moffat.

'Not too close! Halt!' squeals his wife and even Mr Robertson bellows a warning, in a voice, so panicked that I can't even make out the words. We stop in our tracks, bumping and juddering. We come to a wobbly standstill inches from the wagon. Professor Moffat's smile has returned and he slinks up to the wagon, lifts a corner to peer in, widens his eyes and, like a ringmaster, pulls the cloth sideways with a flouncing step and gesture. 'Meet your new companion.'

I jump back, and Ishie's intake of breath cuts through the still summer air. Because under the cloth is an iron cage. And behind the bars...

Is a bear.

CHAPTER 13

AN ASSET TO OUR ACT

'What do you think? Is it not magnificent?' Merriweather Moffat looks like a beggar who has been handed a fortune.

Ishie's eyes are fixed on the creature. A strand of her wavy hair is stuck in the corner of her mouth, but she doesn't brush it away

'It's an asset to our act, darling, that's what it is.' Her mother tidies the strand away and leaves her hand on Ishie's shoulder.

I step forward, slowly and carefully, as the dark beast presses its pointy nose through the bars. I have seen a dancing bear once before, but that bear's nose had been bored through by a heavy metal ring, and its keeper pulled on it with a chain while prodding the poor beast with a stick. That bear's fur was coming out in clumps and its eyes were cloudy.

This bear's nose is shiny and wet, and its glossy fur flickers as it reflects the sun.

'Does it have a name?' I whisper.

Merriweather Moffat wrinkles his nose. 'The trader called it Jack, but I'm sure we can do better than that. It needs to be grand, and impressive, and memorable. I'll think on it.'

With this he strides away, pointing out the way to Mr Robertson. 'A little more over here, if you don't mind, Mr Robertson. Before we move on to you-know-where.' He winks.

What a company we are: an almost-fire raiser, a criminal, a bear, a near-drowned pup and three travelling entertainers. We follow the cage-on-wheels until it reaches its destination below the high trees on the edge of our camp.

And as we all stand beside it, admiring the shiny fur and the glossy eyes and the imposing presence of this new asset to our act, it happens: an almost musical, high-pitched yelp, emanating from my jerkin. Professor Moffat tenses. 'What was that?' he asks sharply.

I feel the pup wriggling and sense the noise before it comes. A squeak, impossibly high. Mrs Moffat leans forward towards the cage. Like her, Professor Moffat does not take his eyes off the bear. 'There is something wrong with the beast, listen! I knew it—it was too good a price! The trader said he wanted the bear to go to someone who would treat it well. And I fell for it!'

'It looks entirely healthy to me, dear.' Mrs Moffat steps forward and almost touches the bars behind which the shiny coat of the bear ripples with every movement. I take my chance to turn around, hoping to re-arrange my jerkin, but accidentally dislodge the wriggling pup. He slides down into my breeches and I give a high-pitched yelp of my own.

'That was Phin! Phin, what kind of noise was that supposed to be?' Ishie demands.

Mrs Moffat sounds concerned. 'Phineas, why in the world are you moving like that? Are you… dancing?'

My face reddens, but I simply can't help it—I dare ANYONE not to wriggle at least a little when a puppy slides down your leg inside your breeches and gets caught at the bottom. It begins to lick my knee, and I'm defeated, collapsing and wrestling my breeches off.

'Phineas!' Mr Robertson is properly alarmed. 'What on God's earth are ye doing?'

'Isn't that obvious?' laughs Mrs Moffat and I like her for smiling and making light of my embarrassment. She picks up the wriggling pup who promptly relieves himself, sending a jet of hot yellow liquid into the summer air.

Merriweather Moffat and his daughter look at each other.

They both look at me.

They look at each other again.

And they all step forward to investigate the bundle in Mrs Moffat's hands. She looks already smitten, and Ishie's face has a tenderness I've not seen before as she leans over to stroke the little ball of fur.

'*Where did you get it?*'

'*Why didn't you say anything?*'

'*Is it a boy?*'

'*Can I hold him?*'

'*Dinnae stroke him too hard! He's only wee!*'

'*How long have you had it?*'

The questions pelt down on me from all sides, but the one comment I expected to hear does not come: 'You have to get rid of it.'

Once the excitement has settled, I get to explain. Mr Robertson curses aloud when I describe that I waded right into the river and earns himself a glare from Mrs Moffat. Ishie holds my wriggling pup gently against her shoulder while her mother fetches more scraps of ham and cold porridge from the caravan.

Professor Merriweather Moffat has remained a little quiet, though, and his eyes flit backwards and forwards between the pup and the bear. He is such a jolly sort that, for a moment, I dared to hope. But surely it is only a question of time before he utters the words I have been dreading. I lower my head and wait.

'There is something I am obliged to say.'

I feel sick.

'Today, I spent almost all of our savings on a dancing bear. I waited till I found a beast well-treated; for all God's creatures are precious. Mark my words, *Professor Moffat's Entertainment* shall be a talking point wherever we go. LOOK at me Phineas!'

With difficulty, I meet his eye.

'And also today, we have gained something else our show was lacking, and free of charge. A live Dog Toby!'

I look at him without seeing. What could he mean?

'Sir, with respect, I don't under...'

'Mark my words! A Punch and Judy opera, delivered with speed and wit, is a success. But a Punch and Judy opera, delivered with speed and wit, AND featuring a trained, live Dog Toby, instead of the puppet? Think on it! This will be an enormous asset to our company!'

I glance from face to face. Ishie translates all the signals I can't read.

'Father saw a show in London with a live Dog Toby; he's always wanted one. Relax! That face you are making is frightful!'

Mr Robertson puts his hand on my shoulder and rubs it, like my father used to do.

The puppy scampers happily between Ishie's and her mother's legs as they sit on the ground, rolling one of Mr Robertson's juggling balls for it.

And I grin down at my dog.

Toby.

CHAPTER 14

THE NAME GAME

'Hercules!'

'A bit foreign, don't you think?'

'Samson?'

'Better. Keep going.'

Since Ishie can't write, the job of recording our suggestions falls to me. The quill's nib has split a little, but no matter. Ishie looks over my shoulder with interest.

'Can I have a turn?'

I look up. 'Erm, yes. Yes! See here, you hold it like this.'

She looks eager, but uncertain. Nevertheless, her movement is almost elegant as she makes a mark in the margin of the paper. Looking up, she asks: 'Any good?'

'It looks a little like a t. Like that letter there.'

She stares at it in wonder. 'T,' she copies me.

'I'll show you if you like. How to write. If I can do it, it definitely won't be too hard for you.'

Ishie smiles and hands the quill back to me, but slowly, as if her fingers didn't want to let go of the feather just yet.

'Think of some more names! They'll be back any minute!'

The midday sun is scattering its rays far and wide when the Moffats approach from their errand in town. Even from a distance I can tell that Professor Moffat is in an excellent mood.

'Tomorrow afternoon,' he belts out as soon as he reaches shouting distance, and he lifts his top hat to let his greying curls blow in the wind. 'It's a market day. And it looks like it's going to stay fair, God-willing!' His face is a sea of joy, and all of us are caught up in its splashes. Over in the field, Mr Robertson is practising bear-tricks, rewarding the beast with fish for each successful attempt. Merriweather Moffat nods approvingly and turns to us.

'And?'

I clear my throat and read out our name suggestions.

There is a moment's silence before all adult voices mingle together.

'Not quite what I was…'

'It's a bear! The name has to inspire respect, not ridicule!'

'Nothing biblical. Don't you think, dear?'

That last statement rules out almost everything else on my list. I scan it through to the bottom. No, Goliath was my last suggestion.

Despite our setbacks, Merriweather Moffat's eyes glow with enthusiasm. 'Come, come.'

He leads us over to the field and points.

'Look at this majestic creature; really look. Take it all in: the shiny fur. The imposing stance, the rippling muscles, the wild eyes. The savage mouth, the fettered power. He needs a NAME. A magic name, a majestic name. Something that heralds: Here is the most awe-inspiring dancing bear in Scotland!'

Professor Moffat drops the ringmaster-voice. 'Not Jack, if you get my drift.'

'The Bruce.'

There is a pause.

I hadn't realised I had said it aloud, still thinking as I was.

'Hmmm.' With each second, a smile is widening on Mrs Moffat's friendly face. 'That does have a ring to it, doesn't it, dear Professor Moffat? Oh, I like it. I like it very much indeed.'

Merriweather Moffat repeats: 'The. Bruce. A creature of battle, and simple enough, hmmm... well, Phineas—I think you have named a bear. And now, no more dallying!' Professor Moffat rubs his hands. 'Let's give The Bruce something to dance to! Phin, fetch the fiddle and the tambourine!'

The following day we arrive at the market square where a corner to the left of the entrance has been reserved for us. Our new wooden sign has been mounted on the iron railing beside:

PROFESSOR MERRIWEATHER MOFFAT AND COMPANY
PUPPETEER, CONJUROR AND BEAR-TAMER
ACROBATICS, MUSIC AND PUNCH AND JUDY'S OPERA
CLOWNING AND STRONG-MAN ACT
NOT TO BE MISSED!

I'm proud of the bear painting beside it, barely dry from when I tried to capture The Bruce's likeness yesterday in the dying light. The more I paint, the more the Moffats give me to do, and I find I enjoy it. Without further ado, Merriweather Moffat projects his voice into the crowd as they arrive in through the gates:

'Gentlemen, do not deny your ladies a marvellous diversion! Fathers, do not deprive your lads and lasses of laughter. Reach deep into your pockets and come close, for what you are about to see, NO man, woman or child has seen before!'

He strikes up a chord on his fiddle and plays as he walks and shouts. Ishie flips this way and that while I help Mr Robertson assemble the puppet fit-up and the small elevated stage for the conjuring tricks.

I hang the puppets, upside down, from the rail inside the booth, in the order in which they will be appearing. Lastly, I stretch out the hat for the money and take a quick peek outside to check on the audience numbers. Ishie is dancing her fiercest jig now, accompanied on the accordion by her mother. There must be at least fifty people here already, not counting the children for they never have more than a penny or two in their pockets. It's the gentlemen you want. There's one right in the front with a rich-looking coat. How strange that he should be standing ahead of all the little ones. No matter, as long as he pays good money. It's as I creep back into the booth to test the curtain, something clicks into place in my brain, and I scramble out backwards once more.

That coat…

I have seen it before. And as I peer carefully through the tiny curtain gap, the realisation lands like a physical blow.

Uncle Ewan is standing in the front row. There are no more than three yards between us.

Suddenly, the fabric draped over the booth seems terribly flimsy to me.

CHAPTER 15

PUNCH

I close the curtain again, trying to breathe, and failing. The applause for the bear roars in my ears and pulses with my pumping blood. What is he, of all people, doing here, of all places? There is only one answer.

Uncle Ewan can't see me. But he'll be able to hear me—more than half the lines in the Punch and Judy opera are mine. I'm seven different characters.

Peeking through the stage curtain is risky, but I cannot resist the temptation. It's him, unmistakeable. Now that I look more closely, Uncle Ewan seems to be handing out some sort of tract. But he was never the religious sort—he left that to Miss Garrow. Oh no, he's turning towards me! I duck down barely in time, my heart beating like a steam locomotive. I jump when the perspiring Merriweather Moffat enters the booth from behind.

'Make some room there, Phin,' he whispers. 'Mrs Moffat is about to announce us. Isn't it a great crowd?'

He is a natural showman. There is pure joy in his

countenance, whereas I feel that the gates of hell are slowly opening beneath me, just as they will for Mr Punch in our play.

Ishie plucks some chords on her harp and the clear, low voice of Mrs Moffat lifts above the murmur.

'Ladies and Gentlemen of Perth, the best and handsomest town of the Great British Empire...'

She says that wherever we go, but still, the audience cheer their assent—and they might even dig deeper into their pockets.

'Children of the finest families Scotland has ever seen. Let us introduce you to the most villainous villain of all: Mr Punch.'

Uncle Ewan is here. Uncle Ewan is here. He is here.

Merriweather Moffat nudges me.

I don't move.

The Professor nudges me hard and I realise: of course! It's my job to pull the chord for the curtain. The showman pops the swazzle into his mouth, wriggles it up into his palate and raises his Punch-puppeted hand high into the stage window.

'Good afternoon, everybody. But halt—why should I bid you a good afternoon when you haven't as much as given me sixpence yet? I'm Mr Punch after all, I don't owe anybody anything. Least of all my quarrelsome wife and my troublesome baby, don't you agree?'

It's my cue and I raise Judy high, clutching the Baby which Punch will hurl into the crowd to the loudest squeal I can muster. Up to this day, my attempts to voice Judy have been passable, but today I cast off the twelve-year old boy and become the shrieking, disapproving and provocative spouse. The Baby flies into the crowd and our carefully choreographed fight takes place, resulting in Judy's daily demise once again. I drop Judy to the ground and wriggle my hand into the Policeman, about to become Punch's victim number three.

Professor Moffat gives me an approving nod during his next Punch-monologue—he must have noticed that my character voices are delivered with much more conviction today. If only he knew why. I imagine Uncle Ewan, leaning forward to see. What does he know? Have I been recognised?

'Oh, and here he comes—the humble servant of the law. Well, he'll be no match for me, I'll wager,' Mr Punch sneers and I wonder how the swazzle can alter Professor Moffat's voice as much as that.

My pitch drops into the lowest cellar of depth. 'Mr Punch. A word please...'

For the first time, I realise that those very words were part of the conversation I would most like to forget in the world. When I was a small, thin boy, waiting beside a hat stand by the door while my father pleaded with the wealthy butcher. *"Mr Finlayson. A word please."*

Punch avoids the question and is chased up and down the stage, as we have rehearsed a hundred times. The audience laugh louder and louder, our puppets pass each other faster and faster, Ishie beats the drum as she always does. They laugh at Punch's witty remarks every time the Policeman goes the wrong way... and with a cymbal-accompanied crash, the fight commences. Now I remember my words!

'Look here Mr Punch!' My voice is deep and it sounds almost like my father. I realise with a shiver that it's not only my next line in the script. It's a memory.

"Look here, Mr Finlayson, my wife is gravely, gravely ill. I beg you to reconsider. Man to man, I am begging you..."

Father sways, but I don't dare stand beside him in the bright light of the hall.

"Think again, Finlayson—her blood will be on your hands. You have the means of preventing her death. With our Lizzie gone and Phineas still young—we need her, Mr Finlayson. Think of your soul, man, and lend me the money for a doctor, I'm begging you! I'm begging..."

"If you wish your wife to have treatment, pay for it yourself! Now Miss Garrow, if you could show the Reverend MacFadden out, please."

My father, so temperate and self-controlled, and a man of the cloth, turns as if to make for the door, but twists round in a sudden, jerky movement and runs up the stairs two steps at a time. There are more words, and then...

The punch lands so hard that I recoil, even at the memory. So loud that the tiny me at the bottom of the stairs staggers back as if I had been struck myself.

The Policeman fights valiantly, as he does every show-time. I hear Uncle Ewan's voice among the ecstatic crowd; his laughter pierces like prongs into my very soul. Mr Punch's baton rains down blows on my Policeman, and even though it's a wooden head, I feel the pain in my hand. A splinter flies, part of the Policeman's helmet. Something to fix and paint over tonight, ahead of the next show, the next fight. If only my father could have been so easily fixed.

A figure, momentarily hanging in the air, swaying at the top of the wide wooden staircase. Teetering backwards. The tiny boy stretches out his hands, as if he could prevent the crunching of bones and the crashing of wood against skull. Soundlessly calling out to his father for the last time in this world.

The Policeman safely dispatched, Punch tricks my Hangman puppet to put his own neck in the noose and the audience laugh and cheer at his villainy, knowing full well he'll get his comeuppance in a moment. I slip the Devil figure on my hand, imitate the rasping lilt of the devil voice and lead Mr Punch to his eternal destiny. My own maniacal laughter surprises even me. I have barely dragged Punch downwards to Ishie's frenzied drumbeat when applause hits me through the thin cloth like a solid wall. Professor Moffat is drenched in sweat, but his eyes gleam. 'Well, well done, Phineas!' he shouts into my ear, loud enough to make himself heard over the noise of the rapturous crowd. 'Very well done indeed.'

But I have sunk down on my knees, hugging myself inside the tight booth.

'Come, come; take a bow!'

All I can do is shake my head. As soon as he steps out, the applause rises once more, and I make a run for it. Away from the market place, along the river and back to camp, into the shelter of the wagon, not looking back once. I don't slow my breathing until I have Toby clutched to my chest.

CHAPTER 16

Things That Happened and Things That Didn't

Mr Robertson comes into the shelter an hour later and I am ashamed I have fallen asleep in the middle of the afternoon. He wakes me gently; his low voice a rumble of comfort. 'Phineas. Wake up.'

'What is it?' I mumble sleepily and Toby squeaks when I uncurl myself. It takes a few seconds for me to sort my thoughts into two neat piles: things that happened and things that didn't.

Uncle Ewan really is here, in Perth.

I escaped. At least for the moment.

The distant memory of the stairs. Yes, that too is true. A well-concealed truth, banished from my mind these many years.

'Here, drink this.' Robertson still has his clowning paste on his face, but his moustache bristles through. 'Phin, this is important. There was a man there in the audience, wi' a right fancy coat, at the front. Did ye know that man?'

Robertson's face is serious, but my discovery would spell danger for him too. My silence confirms his suspicions.

'Be honest wi' me.'

'That man,' I haltingly start, 'is Mr Finlayson—the man I call Uncle Ewan. He is...' I swallow hard. 'He is my guardian.'

'Ah. That explains it.'

'Explains what?'

Mr Robertson leans forward, pulling a crumpled pamphlet from the inside pocket of his coat. My stomach plummets.

'I need tae get back and give them a hand with The Bruce. Dinnae worry. We'll be on our way soon.'

He ruffles my hair kindly. 'We're all on yer side, Phin.'

With that he pulls the canvas across to hide me once more. I wipe my eyes and give Toby a lot of strokes until I can't delay it any longer.

It's a single sheet of paper, folded. On the front is a drawing of a boy who, I realise with near-amusement, is probably meant to be me. Of course, I have never sat for a portrait, and I have certainly never mixed in circles where the new-fangled art of photography could be afforded. I wonder who was tasked with drawing me from memory. No-one ever remembers the delivery boys. I breathe easier.

The print is a little smudged. *Phineas MacFadden. Fireraiser, runaway, ungrateful ward, almost thirteen years of age and of a deceptive, most malevolent nature...* I skip over the first paragraph.

Unconfirmed recent sighting in Perth, by the river at night. The boy is likely to be travelling alone, sheltering under bridges and begging for food.

The corners of my mouth curl up a little, and I allow myself a moment to play with Toby who has taken a fancy to chewing my lace. However, the next paragraph almost takes my breath away.

Owing to his guardian's exceptional forbearance and fondness despite all the boy's crimes, a reward of ten pounds has been offered for information. Write to Perth or Inverness Police stations at the following…

I drop the pamphlet as if it had stung me, and Toby stops chewing and wags his tail.

Considering what the Moffats could do with such a vast sum of money, there can only be one outcome. Mr Robertson must have said what he did to keep me here; to make sure I don't run. But why show me the leaflet?

To gain my trust, of course!

No, there is no other way.

I snap into action, reaching for a coat, sweeping up Toby, and hurriedly pulling myself upwards. Is any food lying around? It may be my last chance to eat for a few days. But I'm distracted by voices, and footsteps, getting nearer and nearer.

They are upon me.

CHAPTER 17

NO NEED TO RUN

Mrs Moffat whispers as she pulls back the curtain, just as I try to ease myself out underneath the canvas on the other side, Toby in one hand and a chunk of bread in the other. I had forgotten: The Bruce's cage has been moved and now backs right onto our shelter. Mr Robertson is sliding the barred gate shut. He looks genuinely surprised when he realises what I am doing.

'Phin?' He steps towards me. I struggle upright as fast as I can. Which way to run?

'Phineas!'

'They're going to have to make their money some other way! I can't go back. Not to him! Never to him.'

I am almost shouting, but I don't care anymore. Running as fast as I can, I make for the river, beyond which I can make out wooded hills. My best chance.

It doesn't take long before Mr Robertson's long, strong legs catch up with me. I hook left and right, but to no avail. Throwing himself down, his arms close around my knees and I fall, putting out my arms to protect Toby in the front of my jacket. My head hits the ground hard, but I don't have time to dwell on that now. Pushing myself up with one hand, I check on the whimpering pup in my pocket with the other.

'Let me go, Mr Robertson. I beg you.'

To my distress, all three Moffats have joined us and are standing in a sort of circle around me. I try to assess for the weakest link in the chain—I reckon Mrs Moffat will be slowest to react, but physically, Ishie may be easier to get past.

'Phin.' Ishie's voice is soft. 'Phin, if you go out there by yourself now, I'll give you an hour at most. But you are by no means friendless. Or unprotected. Stay, and we'll set off now, Father says, as soon as we can make ready. To get you away.'

Mr Robertson nods earnestly. 'No need tae run anymore, Phin.'

'But… why are you helping me?' It sounds so weak when I say it like that, but it's all I want to know. Why? And such a sizeable reward, I simply don't understand it.

'Without you, I'd have no live Dog Toby. You can't deprive me of an asset like that!'

As if on cue, I feel hot liquid shooting down my shirt. 'Ah! Noooo, Toby!' I groan.

Half an hour later, I am wearing one of Merriweather Moffat's clean shirts. The Clydesdale is harnessed to the caravan, with The Bruce's cage pulled behind. Despite the approaching dusk, we set off east and don't stop until Perth is well and truly behind us. When we pull into a field by the side of the road, Mr Robertson cleans his clown face properly in a nearby stream. Rigging up our wee shelter beside the caravan does not take long, and once the Moffats are engaged in preparing the meal, we sit to guard and stoke the fire.

'Want tae see another thing?' Mr Robertson asks and I nod, teasing Toby with a scrap of ham and holding it just out of reach before letting him have it.

'There. See?' He holds up another paper, bigger than the pamphlet he handed me earlier. It looks more like a public notice, and I realise with horror: that is exactly what it is. Only the likeness of Mr Robertson is excellent, almost like a photograph. And the price on his head is more than double the reward offered for me.

I'm momentarily speechless.

'The Moffats. Do they know?'

'Aye. They've seen it.'

'And what…'

'They are determined: they will not give us up. They say we've been true tae them, and showmen aren't the type of people who should have a lot o' money anyway. But if we are discovered, I've resolved that I willnae drag them into any misfortune. They are noble people, Phineas, the like of which I've never met before. They deserve our gratitude, do ye hear? And we can make it up to them by working really hard.'

I nod solemnly. A glance of mutual understanding passes between us and I reach into my pocket. With one movement, both of us feed our respective papers to the flames, before the Moffats arrive with mugs for a hot brew. The flames shoot up brightly as the papers twist and shrivel in the embers.

'Where are we headed now, sir?' I ask Professor Moffat.

'I can't tell you that, Phineas. Suffice to say that, if all goes to plan, it'll be a place the like of which you have never, ever, seen before.'

He chuckles and wanders off into the darkness to check on The Bruce.

CHAPTER 18

MERRIWEATHER MOFFAT'S AMBITION

We set off again early the next day. Regrettably newspapers are read further east, too, so we lie low, grateful for the Moffats' loyalty. 'Really, why do they do it?' I ask Mr Robertson after another patrol of soldiers has ridden past without incident. 'What do they gain? Think of the money, if they turned both of us in?'

There is a chuckle behind the canvas of our shelter and Professor Merriweather Moffat himself sticks his head in.

'I was just about to tell you that the coast is clear when I heard you. Shall I answer?' His eyes twinkle and he holds my gaze. I squirm. 'It's not that I'm not grateful, sir. But I worry that...'

'That it'll all come to an end? Well, Phineas, you are family now, or as near family as you like. I have a lively puppeteer for an assistant, Ishie has a companion, we have another fiddler. Mr Robertson here has natural comic timing, is one of the strongest and most useful hands I have ever known, and quite the natural bear tamer, too. Phineas, not only do I not wish to betray you, I simply cannot do without the two of you. Don't fret another second. We have more important things to focus our minds on.'

He grins widely and beckons us to come closer, as if to impart a great secret. 'Just between us gentlemen: we are heading east, for a small village called Braemar. In a fortnight, they will celebrate their Highland Games, and I have had correspondence: a Punch and Judy man and his companions will be most welcome. Particularly if he brings a well-cared for dancing bear. But our entire performance, gentlemen, will need to be of the highest quality, you may depend on it. The future of *Professor Moffat's Entertainment* rests on this one day. In fact, there will be one particular audience member on whom we absolutely *must* make an impression. Mark my words.'

Later that evening, I watch The Bruce frolic in the field, tied by a long line to a stake in the ground.

'Ishie, where is Braemar?'

She lifts her head from the exercise book where she has produced a regular and elegant row of the letter 'k'. I take the book from her. 'That's really neat by the way. I took much longer to learn this,' I admit.

'Maybe your teacher wasn't very good,' she deadpans. 'Mine is excellent. Braemar...' she thinks out loud. 'Isn't that near Balmoral? Her Majesty, the Queen Victoria herself, is the patron of the Highland games there, is she not?' She looks up sharply. 'Who has talked of this place?'

'I'm not at liberty to say,' I flounder.

'Come on, Phin, out with it. Has Mr Robertson got business there? Or has my father...'

A flicker must have crossed my eyes, and it's all the confirmation she needs.

'My FATHER! He is taking us to see the Queen! Deny it!'

CHAPTER 19

A REAL LIVE DOG TOBY

Now that the secret is out, we travel and rehearse and travel some more. Mrs Moffat has bought a newspaper which states that the Queen is currently in Wales, but that her departure to Scotland is imminent. In our little shelter propped up against the side of the caravan, Mr Robertson and I whisper our worries to each other in the dead of night. Wanted man, wanted boy. Where we're going, there will be soldiers enough to arrest a hundred Mr Robertsons and a thousand Phins.

'We'll take care, Phineas. No' draw attention tae ourselves.'

'Isn't that a little difficult when you're performing on stage? With everyone looking on?'

'Dinnae worry about me. I'll have the clown paste on my face. Now, are ye going tae let me get any sleep or not?'

The familiar sounds eventually lull me to sleep: The Bruce grunting in his slumber; Mr Robertson's snores; the Clydesdale adjusting its weight sideways and snorting; the rustling of straw all around. And outside, the splashing of the river beside the road and the hoot of an owl. The Queen of the Great British Empire, in a place like this?

It simply doesn't seem possible.

Merriweather Moffat has ambitious plans. He wants us to perfect our current Punch and Judy script, with a longer, much more complex chase sequence at the end. He experiments with various lights and flames for hellfire before giving up in frustration when the fit-up fabric ignites at one corner. He insists on darning the hole himself as 'no-one must notice that it's not brand-new anymore'. Once mended, he insists on washing and pressing the whole affair so that I'm almost blinded by the brightness of the red and white stripes. The weather, which has been dull for a few days, brightens up again and Professor Moffat turns his attention to us. 'Ishie dear, let's do that jump routine one more time. Can you try this dance if I fiddle faster? It may look and sound more impressive if we manage it—oh yes, well done. Good girl. Not even the Queen herself could fail to be impressed by such a dance!'

He brushes his greying locks from his face and wipes his forehead. 'Phineas, have you looked at the new script yet?'

Oh Lord, I nearly forgot, I was so distracted by Ishie's frenzied twirling.

'I'll do it right away, Professor Moffat, sir.'

'Good lad. I'll see how Mr Robertson is getting on with The Bruce. I asked him to try a couple of new tricks, but he wasn't convinced. The bear, that is.' Merriweather Moffat winks and hurries down to the bottom of the field where Mr Robertson is encouraging The Bruce to bow on command, with multiple honeyed treats and chunks of salmon.

I turn my attention to the play. How can we make the text as appealing to the Royal household as possible?

When Merriweather Moffat returns, his face beams once more. 'The bear truly is an asset. He is a marvel, and more than a match for any dancing bears the Queen may have seen, for so many such beasts are ill-treated, and the Queen is most compassionate to the welfare of all God's creatures.'

'Professor Moffat, sir?' I begin. 'I've sort of had an idea. About the script. Would you like to hear it?'

To my astonishment, Professor Moffat would. He nods and wriggles ever more excitedly as I explain. 'So, you see what I mean? Sprinkle the script with details and particulars which the Queen is sure to find diverting? Have Punch steal one of her favourite sweets? Have him kick a person she dislikes? Judy could be cooking her favourite meal? And she loves dogs, does she not? Could we mention...'

Merriweather Moffat actually jumps to his feet at that point. 'Of course, she loves dogs! And a dog she shall have! A real live Dog Toby!'

Now, this was NOT what I had planned.

'But, sir, he is barely four months old. He is too young to perform tricks, surely?'

Merriweather Moffat's eyes shine with royal zeal. 'But don't you see, Phineas? It doesn't matter. Your Dog Toby will be charming, whether he performs or not. What dog-lover could fail to be charmed by a well-groomed pup? Shall we try to write him into the script now?'

I take a breath to answer, but the showman has already bustled off to the caravan to fetch a quill and ink for the alterations. I feel Toby wriggle inside my jerkin and decide to let him run. He scampers around my feet and I think that if he had any sense, he'd dash away and never come back.

All our attempts to convince Toby to bite Mr Punch fail.

'Let's try again,' Merriweather Moffat suggests with waning enthusiasm. But the pup seems to hardly notice the puppet, however hard we try.

'Can he at least bark on command?' Professor Moffat demands, wiping his brow.

I shake my head.

'He is young. And, with respect, sir, three days before the big performance seems a little late to start.'

The showman is undeterred. 'You'll see, Phineas; it will all come good. I have an excellent feeling about this opportunity. I am certain it will be most memorable.'

It is hard not to be swept along by his optimism. But I

fear *memorable* may not necessarily be a good thing. Toby falls asleep beside my straw mattress before I've even put on a nightgown. He is as wiped out as I am.

CHAPTER 20

THE BIG DAY

I emerge from our shelter with a sense of trepidation. Today is the day. Much as I can't wait to see Queen Victoria with my own eyes, I dread the possibility that I might let Professor Moffat down. I also dread the soldiers and the high and mighty folk connected with the Queen, who have travelled so far to join her. Merriweather Moffat has left the papers lying around often enough. This may be a village performance, but with a London audience, spoilt by the famous Mr Wilde's West End theatre productions. A wave of nausea washes over me.

Am I imagining it, or is Mr Robertson reluctant to rise, too? The Moffats, by contrast, are up and about, humming, whistling, singing and dancing around our camp. I set Toby down in the field and watch him do his puppy run between me and The Bruce's cage; backwards and forwards and back again. There is a jealous tightness in my chest. All he does is run, for the joy of it. No fear, no past, no guilt. No care who sees him, or who doesn't. Some way off, Ishie twirls in a dress I haven't seen before.

'Like it?' she pants after about ten pirouettes through the grass towards me.

'Like what?' I pretend.

'Saw you staring.' She has this ability of looking straight at me without looking away. I'm slightly jealous of that, too.

'Very nice.'

'Thanks—I got it as a present from my aunt in Edinburgh. I've been saving it for an extraordinary occasion. And this qualifies, don't you think? The Queen herself...' She gazes into the distance dreamily, a smile playing around her lips.

I rise and button my jerkin before whistling for Toby.

'Phin—you are not going to wear that, are you?'

'What, this?' I glance down at myself. 'I don't have anything else, Ishie. You know that!'

It's clean enough, I'm sure, although my breeches are getting a little short.

'At least let me press your shirt for you—it's so crumpled.' She fingers it with a sharp intake of breath. 'Look! And there is a stain!'

She glares at me as if I had committed high treason.

'In case you hadn't noticed, Ishie; I will remain behind the canvas of the fit-up for most of the day. It's only my hands people will see, either with puppets on them, or Toby in them.'

Inwardly, I am raging. A small stain on my front

surely won't affect Queen Victoria's judgment of *Professor Merriweather Moffat's Entertainment Company*! Besides, the Queen is going to spend her afternoon watching men in kilts throwing logs in the mud, and what have you. She won't be put off by a little dirt.

But as is often the case, I do not get a chance to say any of this. Mrs Moffat, ever the sensible one, is walking towards me. She hands me a drying cloth, a bar of soap and a coat hanger. From it swings a shirt so clean it almost blinds me with its brightness, some adult breeches and a waistcoat which must have, at one time, come with a dinner jacket. 'These were Professor Moffat's when he was younger.'

She hesitates and whispers: 'And slimmer. He wishes you to wear them in honour of the day.'

'But…'

She gives me a meaningful look. 'My husband insists, Phineas.'

Ishie giggles and skips away. I huff a little, take the clothes, hang them from the shelter and head for the river with the soap and the cloth. When I emerge, shivering but clean, I am dismayed to see Mrs Moffat waiting beside the shelter with a whetstone and a knife. She means to cut my hair, and no amount of arguing will dissuade her. As I endure it, I console myself with this: I now look nothing like the boy who ran from the market all those weeks ago.

She finishes by kneading some of Merriweather Moffat's

Rowlands Macassar Oil in to smooth my wavy hair to the side.

A few minutes later, I emerge out of the shelter, combed, dressed, braced and belted like a prince. Mr Robertson has finished applying the white clown paste to his face and has painted in the eyes and mouth. With the Clydesdale harnessed to the bear-cage and the puppet-booth loaded on the cart behind, we are clean and ready.

I lead Toby by a cord which doubles as a lead and collar. At the last minute, Mrs Moffat runs back into the caravan to fetch a purple ribbon and ties it in a bow around Toby's neck. 'It's said to be the Queen's favourite colour,' she explains as she clambers on the seat in front, beside her husband. The rest of us walk.

'They say you never know when Her Majesty is going to appear. We'll need to be set up early, and as near as possible to her Majesty's Royal Pavilion. That way, when there is a break in proceedings, she may honour us with her attention.' Professor Moffat's face is lively with anticipation. He taps the Clydesdale with the long reins so it breaks into a trot.

'Keep up, everyone! We do not want others to take the best places. I have an agreement with the man in charge, but even he won't resist a trader with a fistful of sovereigns. Make haste!' Mr Robertson's long legs eat up the miles, while Toby and I try not to fall behind. Ishie jumps on the cart from behind without her parents noticing and whispers: 'I'll need all my energy to dance later. In front of the Queen!' she adds in a hushed squeal. But Professor and Mrs Moffat are too taken up with their secret discussions to notice.

Mr Robertson, on the other hand, has gone terribly quiet.

'No-one could possibly recognise you, Mr Robertson, sir,' I offer by way of encouragement, and he gives me a small smile.

'I dinnae know what it is, Phineas,' he sighs, striding out towards the beautiful natural lawn to the front of the Old Mar Lodge outside Braemar. 'I have an ill-feeling about this.'

CHAPTER 21

MR ROBERTSON'S ILL FEELING

The Royal Pavilion is being decorated with purple ribands. Every time the security guard isn't looking our way, Professor Moffat motions us to move our stage a little closer to it. 'The Queen is elderly now, you see, Phineas. Most likely she will simply observe it all in from her seat yonder. We must entice her to look our way—and the closer we are, the more chance of that. Now!' he hisses to Mr Robertson who pulls the stage a little forward, turning his back directly, as to not invite further scrutiny of his face.

The showman nods with satisfaction. 'I fear if we try any closer they'll make us pack up altogether. Best to take our chances here, don't you agree? Phineas, Mr Robertson, if you'd be so kind as to set up the booth just there.' He points. 'There, to the left of the stage, and in a diagonal position if you please, so that a good view will be afforded to all in the Royal Party.'

We nod and disperse to our respective tasks: Mrs Moffat negotiates performance times with the organisers and buys refreshments. I slot the sides of the booth together, stretch the pristine material over it and give each puppet a last polish with the cloth before hanging them, in the right order, upside down on the rail. I pick a clean swazzle and rest it in the nook at the side of the booth, ready for Professor Moffat to use as soon as he enters. I check the curtain mechanism and clear my throat, for fear of losing my voice for no reason at all. All the stations for the Highland Games are now set up, and we stop to watch as the first competitors in their colourful kilts arrive. I play with Toby and practise various tunes on the fiddle.

Again and again, I finger the tiny silver thruppences and bigger sixpences Professor Moffat gave me earlier. 'There, Phineas—you've earned them, and here will be as grand an occasion to spend them as ever you'll see.' Squinting at the profile image on the gleaming coins, my pulse quickens. The same Queen Victoria, whose face is on these, will sit on that padded chair yonder, and soon.

Professor Moffat returns to show Mr Robertson where to stake The Bruce for his big moment. The powerful muscles ripple under The Bruce's shiny fur. Did he ever roam free? The beast nuzzles up to Mr Robertson.

I am certain that its fondness is returned. Mr Robertson often takes a walk of a night after the Moffats are settled in the caravan. He sits beside The Bruce's cage, mumbling in a low voice.

'Phin!' Ishie twirls over, boundless energy and enthusiasm practically spraying from her eyes. 'The news is, the Queen shall depart Balmoral at one o'clock, so it will be half past two at the earliest before we see her. Father says we are going to perform once over before she comes, wait for the Royal procession to arrive and then repeat it all. I am positive I will faint this second!'

She allows herself to collapse in an ostentatious fashion before remembering that she is wearing her best dress and jumping up as if she'd been stung by a whole hive of hornets. The crowds are certainly beginning to thicken. Some stretches of the road leading up to Mar Lodge now hold rows of spectators, four deep.

We ready ourselves for the first performance, projecting our voices and making them travel as far as we can. Wealthy couples send us their children and they laugh and giggle at Punch's villainy. I wonder at myself—if I had to speak two sentences together, in front of such a respectable audience, I should manage nothing but a stammer. But here, with only a thin (admittedly, gleamingly clean) cloth between me and them, I perform to the crowd as if I had never done anything else. Mr Robertson demonstrates his new range of tumbles as he collects the donations, and I fancy I can hear the difference between the copper pennies that usually fill our bucket, and the shillings and even gold sovereigns that clink together now.

Merriweather Moffat emerges from the booth, bowing deeper and stretching his arms wider than ever, and the audience clap and cheer while keeping a close eye on the road from Balmoral.

Something stirs. Half past two, and the first carriages begin to arrive: The Duke and the Duchess of Fife, with the Duke sat on the box-seat, holding the ribands himself. Not being accustomed to newspapers, I do not recognise them, but Merriweather Moffat, his wife and all assembled crowds wave their hats as the Duff Highlanders march up to greet them.

More carriages follow: Sir Algernon Something-or other, Lady So-and-so, Major Something-something and their many companions, but my brain is not minded to retain such information. I delight in the sight of all the frocks and coats and starched shirts and silk ties, the like of which I have never seen before—or ever shall, I'm sure.

The pristine blue sky smiles down on us all and bathes the surrounding hills, pine-clad to the summits, in a golden afternoon light. A gentle breeze blows from the West. It is the most extraordinary feeling—I forget that I am a fugitive, I forget about Uncle Ewan, about the fire and even about the stairs on that terrible day. Today, I am nothing more and nothing less than a loyal subject of our Queen, Sovereign Monarch over the Empire. I think Mr Robertson feels the same. Who could be cautious on a day such as this?

Who could be weighed down with care when the Queen of the Kingdom is making her way towards one in a carriage of splendour? I step out to cheer, like all the others.

The first party take their seats in the Royal Pavilion, upholstered in black and gold.

At a quarter past three, a cheer goes up that the Queen is coming, and the excitement of the moment travels, like a physical movement, along the road. In the distance, we spot the red coats of the outriders and Ishie bounces up and down beside me.

'I'm going to faint with the thrill, Phin! The Queen! Queen Victoria herself!' Her voice is nothing but a squeak, soon drowned out by the rising cheer. The Queen's carriage pulls smartly up on the gravelled roadway and halts by the Royal Pavilion, mere yards from where we are standing.

The Duke of Fife rises: 'Bonnets off!' he cries, stepping forward to greet the Queen. There are many, many people with her, but Queen Victoria is unmistakable, emerging as she does in a stripy black gown, which must be silk, a black shiny jacket trimmed with elaborate jet and fringe, and a black and white bonnet.

She is an old woman, but she is the most spectacular sight I have ever, ever, EVER seen. I cheer and whistle so loudly that Mr Robertson nudges me from behind. 'Dinnae attract attention; ye're going tae need that voice for the show!' He melts away again and I clear my throat, worried for a second. Instead of cheering, I wave my cap high in the air—Ishie cheers loudly enough for the two of us anyway.

There are well-to-do families aplenty, with well-to-do children to boot. We wait until the marching has finished and until the toss-the-caber round has come to an end.

When the Queen begins talking to a young lady beside her, holding a cup of tea, Professor Moffat strikes up the fiddle. Ishie takes to the treads, faces the Pavilion, smiles, bows and launches into her first leap, legs almost doing the splits before landing elegantly and showing some of the fastest footwork I have ever seen anyone do. She twirls and, from my vantage point behind the booth, I watch the Queen closely. She nods in response to something the young woman says. Still Ishie spins, faster and faster. Five, six, seven revolutions. Again, I watch the Queen. She is lifting her hand and pointing to Ishie, and the young woman turns around to see, too. Nine, ten—my friend is going to lose her balance for sure! Her leg has shifted from the middle of the platform to very near the edge. *Stop,* I want to shout, but she is possessed, faster and faster and faster and....

Both Mr Robertson and I start towards the stage, but we are too late. Ishie finishes her endless pirouette with an arabesque which hangs in the air for a second—before her foot slides off the edge of the treads. The little platform tips, Ishie staggers sideways and the whole thing clashes to the ground. Merriweather Moffat somehow manages to bring the melody to an instant end, stopping with a strong chord, and Mrs Moffat rushes up to her daughter, before the rest of us can.

I bite my lip, not breathing. Did I hear her ankle crack? It meant so much to her. So much.

Ishie's face is stony as she manages a small curtsey before hobbling sideways and out of view. A quick glance to the Pavilion: The Queen raises her eyebrows in a brief acknowledgement of pity, before turning her attention to the Prince of Wales beside her.

CHAPTER 22

THE ROYAL PAVILION

I'm about to dart after Ishie when Merriweather Moffat stops me.

'Phineas! Where are you going?' He is tense—no jollity in his voice at all.

'Is she…'

'Yes, yes, she'll be fine, I'm sure. It's likely twisted rather than broken. Listen, Phineas; Her Majesty's attention won't be on us for much longer. We need to make an impression, and we need to do it now. See there?'

He half-turns, indicating behind him with his head. 'She glanced over. Let your voice carry, like I taught you. You are a showman, do you hear? You ARE a SHOWMAN. It's what you do.'

He ducks into the booth, pulling me with him, pops the swazzle up into his palate and wriggles Mr Punch over his hand. I can hear the accordion introduction for our play, so Mrs Moffat must be back. Where is the script? My mind has gone blank; completely blank.

'Phineas!'

Oh yes. 'Sorry', I whisper and pull the cord for the curtain as Toby wriggles inside my fancy waistcoat. Professor Moffat projects his high, rasping swazzle-voice so that it carries above the din of the crowd.

'Good afternoon, Your Majesty. May I complement your stripy gown, an elegant choice,' rasps Punch.

'Waaah,' I chime in with my baby voice. The Judy puppet over my hand clutches the Baby in her arms, and I manoeuvre them onto the stage.

'I wonder if the Prince of Wales ever made a noise such as this when he was a wee boy?' Punch exclaims, holding his ears, and I fancy I can hear a man laugh from the Royal Pavilion. No time to peek—I need to make sure Punch can grab the Baby from my Judy without dropping it so that he can hurl it into the crowd.

Delighted shrieks arise from the tightly packed audience: it's working. High on her Pavilion seat, the Queen will have an excellent view.

I move the Judy puppet and squeal: 'Mr Punch, you've killed our BABY! Oh, Mr Punch, I will hit you!'

There is a scuffle, a chase and an exchange of punches with loud whacks of wood on wood. With Judy dispatched, I pull on the Policeman. There is more laughter from the Royal Pavilion as I throw my puppet's neck back and strut around the booth like a peacock. But the best moment of the play is when I wriggle Toby out of my sleeve. It takes both of my hands to hold him up at the right level so that he can be seen clearly, but my hands cannot. There is a collective "*aaaaw*" from the audience and, drenched in sweat, Merriweather Moffat gives me a sideways glance of pure glee inside the booth. To my relief, Toby does exactly what I hoped. Before the show, I smeared Punch's nose with beef-stock, and just as planned, Toby not only licks Mr Punch's face; he actually closes his teeth around Punch's huge nose and wrestles, play-growling all the while.

'I say, do look at that!' a woman's voice from the Royal Pavilion exclaims. 'That dog is adorable!'

We enact the chase, and Toby barks sharply, until Mr Punch grabs our stuffed replica, made of dyed fur, and shakes it at lightning speed. The audience gasps before realising they have been tricked. Punch hurls it into the crowd, too, and there is spontaneous applause for such drama.

With Toby safely back into my deep jacket pocket, I take a breath. Most of this final section is about the chase anyway. The accordion music gets faster and faster while I run my puppet left to right, left to right, right to left, clash in the middle, pop up stage right, pop up stage left…

I almost recite the movements to myself as I execute them, like a carefully choreographed dance. There is doubtless joy as Professor Moffat and I move together and apart, turn our puppets away and towards each other, emanating shrieks and hollers and shouts. When Punch is finally hurled into hell, even the accordion is drowned out by the cheers and the applause. As agreed, Professor Moffat and I step out and bow, and of course our very first glance takes us to the Queen. She is clapping.

Clapping!

The Queen of the British Empire is clapping for me.

My bow is so low and I bounce up so straight that I could bounce right out of this universe with happiness.

After much handshaking and waving and collecting, our hat is full to bursting with heavy coins—and then I remember Ishie.

Where is she?

I can't ask Mr Robertson, because he and Professor Moffat are erecting a small barrier to separate the audience from the beast—although I'm sure it would make little difference if either party were determined to breach it.

Ishie, where are you?

Ah, there! My friend sits hugging her knees at the edge of the lawn, alone.

'You did well,' she says before I have even reached her. 'That was the best show you and Father have ever given.'

'Look Ishie, I'm so…'

'It was perfect, Phin. Perfect. I knew what was coming, and I was still engrossed. And her Majesty the Queen watched you all the while—I noted she didn't glance away once. A triumph!'

She doesn't meet my eye, but stares straight ahead. The beautiful dancing gown is smeared with grass, mud and disappointment. Her hair hangs across her face like a broken theatre curtain, but thank heavens, her eyes are dry. I haven't the first idea what to do with crying girls. I breathe a little more easily and put my hand on her shoulder, before realising what I am doing and pulling it back.

'Where has your mother gone?'

'Fetching ice from the big house—it's likely that they will have some.'

We are distracted by the crowd. There is a break in the competitions and Mr Robertson has led The Bruce onto the stage. Once the huge animal rears up to its full height on its hind legs, we can easily make him out, even from this distance. What would the Queen say if she knew that our bear was named after a rebel who defeated her ancestors centuries ago? I don't imagine anyone will go out of their way to tell her.

Ishie rubs her ankle. It is swollen, but not so swollen as I had feared.

'Can you put weight on it at all?'

'I don't know. I'm fearful to try. Oh, Phin; if I can't dance, I can do nothing.' Her voice cracks a little at the last sentence. I stretch myself up and offer my hand.

'I'll help you up. Slowly and gently.' I try to smile.

'I suppose. But careful, Phin—I'm heavier that you think.' She smiles with one corner of her mouth, which must be a good sign.

'I'll be the judge of that,' I quip and pull her upright. She does wince a little, but is able to move her foot round and round, slowly. She gingerly stands on both legs, and (only for a second) pulls her healthy leg off the ground and lets her bad ankle hold her weight. She lifts her eyes and smiles with both corners of her mouth.

Mrs Moffat bustles across the field, thrusting a heavy package of ice into my arms. 'Hold this for a second, if you'd be so kind, Phineas. Now, Ishbel, sit again, and elevate the leg like this. That's right. It's not so very bad, my girl, it'll mend. And sooner than you think. Thank you, Phineas, that will do.'

She shrugs off her shawl, distributes the ice liberally on it and winds it around her daughter's ankle. Ishie's face has fallen again. 'My one chance,' she mutters. 'My one chance to dance in front of Queen Victoria. And what do I do? I fall over.'

Her bottom lip begins to quiver.

'No use dwelling on it, darling girl. You may dance in front of royalty yet; you've a long life ahead of you, I hope.' Mrs Moffat is brisk and efficient. 'Just you lie back here and look up for a bit. There's nothing that can cheer one up quite the same as a blue sky overhead, and the sound of a happy crowd. Come, Phineas. I fear we are both needed.'

She beckons, marching off in the direction of the dancing bear and its crowd, now on their feet and clapping along to Merriweather Moffat's fiddle music. The Bruce is twirling on his hind legs, pawing the air in front with his great claws.

'The stupid bear can do it, and I can't!' spits Ishie before I'm quite out of earshot.

CHAPTER 23

WHISKY

That night at camp, we all sit together around a tray of royal leftovers, gifted to us by the Mar Lodge kitchen. A fallen tree covered with blankets serves as a bench, and Ishie can put her leg up on it. We don't tell her Toby relieved himself against it seconds before she took her seat.

The Queen left at six o'clock, waving cheerfully to all of us, though the competitions continued for some time after. We packed everything up and headed back to the caravan at around seven, ahead of Merriweather Moffat who had some business to attend to. After seeing to The Bruce and cleaning everything up properly, we unwrap the great trays of sandwiches, cold meats and every good thing, and even Ishie recovers a little from her low mood.

When Professor Moffat arrives on the back of a passing cart, he pulls out a bottle from his coat and joins us.

'This day has been momentous. I do not purchase whisky for nothing. But in the history of our little company, today has been momentous indeed!'

I shift uncomfortably in my seat and eye the bottle. Uncle Ewan had one like it. When he was still Mr Finlayson to me.

The glugging of the amber liquid into Mr Robertson's mug takes me back, however hard I fight it, to being a small boy, cowering in the shadows by the door at the foot of the stairs.

My father the Reverend standing at the bottom, Ewan Finlayson at the top like an evil giant, about to hurl lightning from on high.

"Look here, Mr Finlayson, my wife is gravely, gravely ill. I beg you to reconsider. Man to man, I am begging you!"

Father sways, but I don't dare stand beside him in the bright light of the hall.

"Think again Finlayson—her blood will be on your hands. You have the means of preventing her death. With our Lizzie gone and Phineas still young—we need her, Mr Finlayson. Think of your soul, man, and lend me the money for a doctor, I'm begging you! I'm begging…"

"If you wish your wife to have treatment, pay for it yourself! Now Miss Garrow, if you could show the Reverend MacFadden out, please."

The housekeeper steps forward. My father, so temperate and self-controlled, and a man of the cloth, turns as if to make for the door, but twists round in a sudden, jerky movement and runs up the stairs two steps at a time.

"Mr Finlayson, my wife has worked for you for nigh-on

a decade, with diligence. I have paid for all the treatment myself, and my funds are simply exhausted. You know I have nothing left, and that the kirk doesn't give out loans. You know that. The doctors are saying that, with more treatment, she may yet recover. Has she not been a diligent employee, Mr Finlayson? Tell me!"

"You are mistaken, Reverend, if you think I have funds to spare to squander on every man, woman and child who has ever been in my pay. Miss Garrow…"

My father looks so slight in his shabby frock coat as he squares up to the taller man. "You are our only hope, Mr Finlayson. She is not long for this world. We have prayed, we have… but she is fading."

"Then I suppose that is the way of the world. If her time has come, accept it, Reverend. You of all people should know that."

"But it is in your power to help. In YOUR power."

The men are nose to nose, Finlayson's broad shadow swallowing up that of my father, all the way down the stairs.

"My answer is no, Reverend. Now begone!"

The movement is tiny and lightning-fast: Father's fist shoots up towards the butcher's face who catches it easily. But Father's other hand grabs the tall man by the collar. Finlayson's huge fist lands on my father's forehead with crushing accuracy. I am glued to the spot as my father tumbles down the stairs. Thumping and cracking and splitting and breaking sounds echo in my head. The man that was my father lies motionless at the bottom of the stairs. At the top, Mr Finlayson loosens his collar.

"Now get up and get out of my house."

Nothing moves.

"Get out! Now!"

Still silence.

Miss Garrow rustles forward. "Sir."

"What?"

"He doesn't appear to be breathing."

Mr Finlayson stands stock still for a moment. Then he calmly walks into the upper hall. I hear clinking noises, and a second later he comes down the stairs with a bottle of whisky in his hand.

"Speak to no-one of this, for as long as you live." He doesn't look at Miss Garrow, simply feels the wrist and the neck for a pulse and pulls at my father's eyelids as if he was a doll. Finally, he yanks back my father's head, opens his mouth and pours at least half the bottle of whisky down his throat. Miss Garrow makes a little noise and looks away.

Ewan Finlayson is not finished: he splatters whisky over the front of my father's shirt, waistcoat and coat.

"There. Drunk he was. Out of his mind. Made a public nuisance of himself, threatened me and fell down the stairs. Understand?"

He lifts his hand and steps towards the housekeeper.

"Understand?"

She edges backwards. "Yes, yes, I understand." Her eyes flit to eight-year-old me, trying to melt into the hat stand by the door.

"But, sir—what about the boy?"

There is a pause.

"What boy?" His voice is bubbling low.

"Tha... that boy, standing there. The Reverend's boy."

The butcher's calculating eyes rest on me for a long, long time.

'Would you care for some cocoa, Phineas? You are miles away in your thoughts.' Mrs Moffat's smiling face is close to mine, and I am pulled back into the here and now. The warm cocoa from her pan does smell tempting. She presses a tin cup into my hand and begins to pour. Then she stands back. 'You look a little ill. Don't you think Phineas looks a little unwell, Merriweather?'

'I am quite well. I was only thinking of something unpleasant.' I shrug.

Mr Robertson's gaze lingers on me with an intensity I find uncomfortable, so I add: 'Today was quite an occasion, was it not?'

This seems to have the desired effect. Everybody joins into the chorus of exclamations again, although Ishie stays quiet. Professor Moffat swirls the drink in his glass and holds it high.

'And now I come to the best news of all.'

We look at him intently.

He puts his whisky glass on the crate serving as a table, pulls over my mug of cocoa, and wriggles a spoon between them to create a drum roll. We all laugh.

'Her Majesty the Queen's Secretary stopped me after our performance and asked...'

It is typical of Professor Moffat to make us wait in anticipation.

'And asked if we'd be so kind as to perform in front of the Queen and her guests in Balmoral's walled garden, Thursday next.'

The crackle of the fire is the only sound, apart from the rustle of the leaves in the wind. Even The Bruce's usual grunts are absent. Ishie is first to recover. 'I get another chance to dance in front of the Queen?'

'It looks like it, my dear, providing your ankle heals and the weather stays fair.' For a moment, he looks emotional. 'We may now paint the word "Royal" on our advertising, Mr Robertson, for we have performed in front of Royalty. I am a very, very fortunate man.'

Mr Robertson raises his glass. 'Tae *Merriweather Moffat's ROYAL entertainment company!*'

All of us repeat the toast and clink our tin cups against his.

It is very late before I am sent to check on The Bruce while Mr Robertson makes the fire safe for the night.

In the dark, I carefully trace my way along the caravan to reach the cage. The beast normally breathes much more heavily than this. I narrow my eyes and concentrate hard on listening. There is almost no light now. Feeling my way cautiously along the bars, there is a little creak. My heart stops.

Impossible! There should be no creaking. Unless…

A retch rises in my stomach. The open gate of the cage is swinging gently in the breeze.

There is no sign of our bear.

CHAPTER 24

THE HUNT

My heart beats faster than Punch's baby's rattle. *Deep, deep breaths, Phineas; there's nothing to be gained by having a heart attack. Who was here last?*

With a further plummet of my stomach I wonder: *was it me?* I helped Mr Robertson give The Bruce his last feed. I was the one who closed the gate.

Didn't close the gate, apparently. And Mr Robertson checked the gate after me. *Or did he?*

In the dark, I can barely make out the wooded hills; The Bruce could be anywhere by now, up any of those trees. Anywhere!

But I have stood here too long!

'The Bruce is gone.' I say it quietly, like a dress rehearsal, before stumbling towards the camp. 'The Bruce is gone! THE BRUCE IS GONE!'

Mr Robertson emerges first, struggling to pull on a coat. 'What?'

I explain. Or I try, for he talks over me almost immediately.

'I knew that lock wasnae safe! I told the Professor it needed seen to!' He mumbles a series of curses, and I flinch at the ungodliness. Turning away, I close my eyes and send a desperate prayer to heaven. *May the bear be found. May Merriweather Moffat not be angry...*

That last prayer takes a bit of believing.

The entertainer emerges out of the caravan, struggling into his clothes. 'How could this possibly have happened! Was it sabotage?'

'I dinnae think so. That lock has needed replacing ever since we got The Bruce, Professor Moffat.'

Moffat emanates some sort of groan, and Mrs Moffat places a calming hand on his shoulder. 'Dear. Is it perhaps wise to wait until morning?'

He shakes her off impatiently. 'And have the whole regiment on our heels? Did you see how many soldiers were here today, dear? Do you think they would dream of permitting our performance at the Queen's residence if there was the slightest doubt of our competence? The slightest hint of danger? I think not!' He lifts a burning branch from the edge of the fire, holds it above his head like a torch and marches off towards the empty cage, slamming the creaking gate shut.

'This is hardly helpful!' Mrs Moffat mutters.

I wonder if Mr Robertson is thinking what I am thinking. Newspaper headlines and investigators and soldiers and sheriff officers. Questions. We need to find that bear, for more reasons than one.

Professor Moffat is all bustle and panic, while the calm voice of Mrs Moffat gives us the thing we crave the most: something to do.

'Mr Robertson, would you be so kind as to fetch the rope tied to the back of the caravan. Ishie… Ishie?'

'Here, mother.' Her voice is sleepy, but she hobbles towards us as fast as she can manage, wrapped in a shawl and a blanket.

'The Bruce has…'

'The bear seems to have…'

'That lock hasnae been right…'

'I know, I know. I heard!' she cuts us short. 'I'm sure they heard in China, with all the racket you are making.'

Merriweather Moffat takes a deep breath, probably to scold her for her disrespect, but he thinks better of it. His wife, meanwhile, continues.

'Ishie, there is a box with meat for The Bruce under the caravan. You know the one. Fetch and wrap it; your father and Mr Robertson must take it with them. And let's have a light—there are three lanterns in the caravan. Trim them anew, and quickly—you can see to that Phineas. We may be able to make out the beast's prints in the mud and learn of the general direction he took. I will check the river—it is salmon season, is it not? I'll be back directly.' Her portly figure disappears over the field towards the glittering stream.

'Yes, dear. Yes, that appears to be a wise course of action.' Merriweather Moffat's voice trails away. His wife returns soon, shaking her head.

Light and ropes assembled and food gathered, the adults decide to set off for the woods, for the imprints on the mud lead that way. Mrs Moffat puts a hand on each of our shoulders. 'Ishie, Phineas, you must stay here. Guard the horse, and keep the fire alight. The glow will help us navigate our way back. It may take us all night to find the bear. And find him we must.'

CHAPTER 25

A SHAPE IN THE NIGHT

The three little dots of their lanterns soon disappear into the looming hills. They call for the bear, but softly, waving salmon and listening keenly. We see them separate in the distance as agreed: Merriweather and Alice Moffat head towards the Old Mar Lodge, while Mr Robertson goes alone in the opposite direction.

I am vexed. Surely, Ishie could guard the camp on her own! I sigh, put Toby in his crate and step outside.

No birdsong, no hoofbeats on the road, and very little light, for the moon is a narrow slither, often obscured by passing clouds. A knot begins to form in my stomach. The Bruce could have gone for miles by now, in any direction at all. Bears are masters at concealing themselves in dense woods, I'll be bound.

The Clydesdale grazes a little way off, its silhouette just visible against the sky in the dim moonlight.

'What would we do, if the bear returned?' Ishie asks.

'I don't know,' I admit. All seems calm. The horse flares

its nostrils but then lowers its head again to feed.

My eyelids begin to droop. Occasionally, Ishie nudges me when she fancies seeing a flash of faint light in the distance, but I am beyond caring. The soft rustle of the treetops above lulls me to my dreams.

'Phin! Phin! Wake up!'

Ishie is on her feet and directs a proper kick at my side.

'What…?' I struggle upwards.

'Shhhh!' She points. The Clydesdale stands in the middle of the field, the tether at its full stretch. Its head is raised; its ears are back, twitching.

'There is something there,' she whispers.

The horse whinnies and shies, trotting across and tugging the rope the other way.

'Something is coming, from over there. From the river.'

We both know what that something is.

The Bruce is tall for a black bear, and although he walks on all fours, in this light, I'm not surprised that the horse is beside itself with fear. My own heart is beating so hard, it might burst right out of my chest. The horse paces back and forth, but the bear moves towards it, slowly and deliberately.

'We have to set the horse loose,' Ishie whispers in a horrified croak.

'Would The Bruce attack the horse? Surely not!' The Clydesdale is huge.

133

But it's also tied, and this bear must be hungry. Ishie and I stand helpless. Where is Mr Robertson when you need him?

'We have to get him back into his cage,' whispers Ishie behind me.

'We must make sure he doesn't attack the horse,' I whisper back. 'Distract him.'

'With what?' she mouths.

I eye the bulky silhouette. Along the field, the Clydesdale moves skittishly, ears flat against its head.

'Do we have any of the bear's feed left?' We both know the answer: the adults took all we had left. And where they are now, no-one knows.

'Wait!'

An idea crosses my mind. A silly idea, but it's the best I have.

'Give me a moment, Ishie!'

I sprint back to the caravan. Seconds later I emerge again, carrying the leftover platter of royal food from that afternoon.

Slowly, slowly I edge around the horse. 'Untie the Clydesdale, Ishie,' I call over my shoulder, not taking my eyes off the black bear for fear of losing sight of him in the dark.

'There you are, Bruce...' I try to imitate Mr Robertson's deep, soothing voice. I have a feeling the bear won't fall for it though.

The Bruce stops, pushes himself up on his hind legs and raises his nose high in the air. My courage nearly fails me. Behind me, I can hear the low thuds of hooves on the ground: Ishie is leading the Clydesdale towards the caravan, talking in a low voice. Now there is nothing between The Bruce and me; nothing AT ALL. The bear's eyes glint whenever the moonlight catches them. An owl hoots and the bear drops on all fours again, beginning to slap the ground in front of him. I've seen his giant paws, and the claws which now churn up the dark grass, close up. Without meaning to, I back away, only to realise—if I retreat, he may not follow. I need him to follow. A quick glance over my shoulder. It's useless. I can't see anything anyway.

But something happens that I didn't expect. The Bruce coils back his top lip, raises his mouth towards me, paws the ground harder and harder, blowing air out of his nostrils in a strange kind of rhythm.

And then…

He charges.

CHAPTER 26

BOY VERSUS BEAR

I find myself sprinting full pelt towards his cage, trying (and failing) to balance the plate of royal delicacies. Crustless sandwiches and cold ham strew the field, but I care little.

I reach the creaky gate and wheel round, but The Bruce is not behind me anymore.

With the horse tied to the other side of the caravan, my friend returns.

'He was bluffing.' Ishie's voice brims with wonder. And she is right. The bear is behaving normally now. No blowing, or slapping. Snout to the ground, he is helping himself to Queen Victoria's leftovers.

Suddenly, he raises his head and takes a step towards us. *Uh-oh.*

No, he bends down again. And then, at last, I know what to do.

'Ishie, we have to back away.'

I hurriedly scrape together all of the Queen's ham left on the platter. Down it goes, all of it; down on the ground in a messy line between bear and cage. As we back around the corner and out of sight, I hurl the final pieces into the cage, making sure a couple of meaty morsels land on the ramp. Ishie, meanwhile, pulls open the gate as wide as it will go and squeezes herself in behind it. 'Yes!' is all I have time to whisper before darting to a nearby tree and hiding behind it. Good, the wind is blowing in my face. That means The Bruce will not be too distracted by my scent. I can hear Toby growling his pathetic little growl in the shelter, but even he wouldn't be mad enough to come out when there is a huge black bear on the prowl.

Both Ishie and I stand statue-still. The Bruce is out of sight, but we can hear his snorting and chewing. He seems to be getting closer.

The bear's huge head appears around the corner of the open cage and I produce an involuntary gasp. The gate (with Ishie behind it), wobbles a little. One by one, the huge paws appear and pad down on the soft ground. The moon picks this very moment to make an appearance from between the clouds and outlines the giant animal in all its ghostly glow. The Bruce lifts his head and sniffs intently. Oh no. The wind has turned.

The bear takes a couple of steps towards me. Can I climb my way out of this? Not likely; black bears are excellent climbers. But The Bruce has dropped to his fours again and investigates the meat on the ramp.

Ishie must know that the bear is only inches from her, but she can't see him for the door. At this angle, she must be able to see me though, so I hold my hands out in a warning gesture.

Wait.

Wait.

Wait.

The Bruce licks the ramp and lifts his head, peering in.

Then, with a movement that shakes the whole cage, he leaps inside.

'NOW!' I shout, sprinting forward. Ishie and I push the door shut with all our strength before realising the fatal flaw in our plan: there is no lock or bolt. It's all broken away. I curse myself for being so stupid. That's why The Bruce escaped in the first place!

'Now what?' she grunts, leaning against the door with all her weight. Her ankle must hurt.

'Can you hold it on your own for a second? I'll try to find something we can use. Those screws on either side—we could maybe tie something to them?'

I sprint towards the caravan and return with rope, wire and wood kindling. The Bruce paws the door and we jump back every time the door bangs and wobbles, but eventually we manage to wedge, tie and bind it shut enough to be able to step back.

'Do you think it's safe?' I whisper, out of breath.

'Who knows?' she answers. 'But I can't think of anything else we can do. I'll take the horse back to the field to graze. And then I'll sleep.'

She sways a little and has to steady herself against the caravan.

'Let me tend to the horse, Ishie. Rest your foot for Thursday.' I nod encouragingly and vaguely motion towards the caravan, but she looks puzzled. 'Thursday?'

'Thursday,' I repeat.

Outlined against the light in the caravan, she mumbles dreamily: 'Oh yes. That.'

She hobbles away without even saying goodnight and I hear no noise from the caravan, so I suspect she has gone to sleep as she was, still dressed in her overcoat.

The fire has almost gone out, so I quickly build a criss-cross of new branches and lie down low to blow into the embers. Scraping together the last few crumbs on the platter, I take a mouthful and sit beside the dancing flames until I feel something move at my feet. Poor Toby! He must have been terrified.

The pup prods me with his nose until I scoop him up into my lap. With each stroke down his smooth fur, some of the tension leaves me. I say another prayer, for the Moffats and Mr Robertson to make it safely back. It isn't until dawn that they come.

All three look dejected. They slump back beside me.

'Well done for staying awake, Phineas,' Mrs Moffat says, patting my shoulder. 'One of us can stand guard now. We'll need to report it, so there is probably no point in going to bed anyway.'

'But…,' I begin, except Professor Moffat cuts me off, rubbing his forehead. 'I'll see to it, dear.' He balls his hands into fists and massages his eye sockets. 'My main concern is that they are sure to impose a fine, at the very least. They may even revoke my licence.'

I try again: 'Sir, can I…'

'And if the bear is spotted, he will certainly be shot.' He groans and turns to us. 'Mr Robertson, Phineas, I think it best if you took a day trip tomorrow, before the investigators call.'

'But Professor Moffat, sir, please listen…'

'No, Phineas. We mustn't risk your discovery, whatever the cost.'

I've had enough. 'THE. BRUCE. IS. IN. HIS. CAGE!' I shout, resulting in a flutter and twitter of roosting birds in the tree tops. 'Ishie and I lured him back in!'

If only I were a portrait painter! The expression on the adults' faces is priceless.

CHAPTER 27

THE REWARD

It being a Sunday, the Moffats and I go to church to give thanks for the return of the bear while Mr Robertson creates a makeshift bar on the gate. The afternoon is spent resting. Ishie keeps her leg up, to give her ankle a good chance of recovery.

I get dressed late the next day. Mr Robertson has already been to the ironmonger's in Braemar and is fixing a new lock onto the gate of the cage. The brand-new metal gleams in the afternoon sun.

The Bruce seems perfectly at ease, staked to the ground by a collar round his neck. No nose-ring. I am glad that our bear is cared for well.

Ishie seems to be limping a little less this morning, and Professor and Mrs Moffat are back to their cheerful selves. Mrs Moffat stops pegging up washing on the line when she sees me and picks up a parcel from the side of the caravan.

'Phineas, come here a moment! I had Mr Robertson fetch

something else from Braemar this morning. I wondered what it was that you needed most, and I didn't have to think for long. A boy like you needs boots, proper adult boots to grow into. They weren't cheap, but you saved us many a fee last night with your quick thinking. You did well, Ishie and you.'

She ruffles my hair and returns to her washing. I stare down at the boots. Leather, like my father's boots. Darker, shinier, newer. Maybe even a little bigger. And from nowhere, I am ambushed by tears. I grab the boots and run towards the trees to be alone, but at the very moment that I shoot past The Bruce's cage, Mr Robertson turns the corner and I crash into him at full speed.

He laughs at first, until he sees my face.

'Phineas, lad, what's wrong? No, dinnae struggle, I'm tryin' tae help.'

He holds me lightly, but doesn't let go either. With a quick glance over his shoulder, he puts his arm around me and leads me towards the trees. I sink onto the mossy roots, clutching the new boots to my chest and allow my heart to break for a minute. Mr Robertson looks distressed, but he doesn't take his eyes off me and rubs my back.

I can't explain. Not to him, can I? Least of all to him.

My eyes travel down to his legs and then his feet. My father's boots. A little more scratched and worn, but strong and lasting.

My father's…

I recoil at the shock—I said that aloud. Mr Robertson's eyes come to rest on the old boots, too, and in this shared moment, I know that we are both back in the tree beside the Sherriff Court in Inverness, with the smoke in the air and the flames whipping high into the sky.

And without words, he seems to understand. He begins to untie the laces. I let my tears flow, only interrupted by the occasional hiccup.

He holds the boots out to me by the laces. 'Yer father's?'

I nod. 'The only thing I have left.' I manage to mumble.

'I am deeply, deeply sorry, Phineas. I didnae realise.' Now he can't meet my eye, and I sense shame like a hound senses blood. I am a Reverend's son after all.

He draws himself up.

'Wait! Take these, Mr Robertson. The Moffats gave them to me, but…'

He hesitates for a very long time. 'Are ye sure now?'

'Certain. And… thank you, sir.'

He shakes his head, as if the word 'sir' was a wasp circling his face. He takes the new boots and walks stiffly back towards the camp. I lie under the tree for a while still, wriggling my toes in my father's boots, letting the redness in my eyes and nose subside; and I realise.

I do love Mr Robertson, as a son loves a father.

The days between now and Thursday are filled with rehearsing. The Bruce has learned to roll over sideways in such a short time and will do it on command for a hunk of fish. Toby bites Punch's head on command, too; as long as he gets a treat. I am so very proud of him. Professor Moffat's grin could not get any broader.

Mr Robertson practises his clown tumbles and does his exercises, for the improved Strong-Man act is the most impressive part of his routine. Late on Wednesday afternoon, Mrs Moffat returns from the village with another parcel and pulls me aside.

'I see that I didn't get the size right for the boots. It was kind of you to give them to Mr Robertson, and to make do with his old ones. Therefore, I've had in mind to surprise you with something better.'

Her face positively glows with anticipation. It's oblong, only wrapped in a piece of rolled up cloth. I take it and place it on the ground to unroll, but she stops me.

'Take care now! It's fragile!' She shakes her head in disapproval, but that is soon wiped away when I fling my arms around her neck, forgetting all propriety. I don't feel like crying this time. I feel like sprinting up the highest hill and shouting so that the whole world may hear it:

I have been given my very own fiddle!

CHAPTER 28

BALMORAL

There is an edge to Merriweather Moffat's politeness early on Thursday morning. The clouds threaten a reappearance after three days of practically clear skies and he does not like it one bit.

'Imagine the weather turning, just as the Queen herself is having a garden party for the grandchildren,' he mutters accusingly, as if the sky didn't know how to behave itself.

Mrs Moffat sighs. 'We'd better go, or else we'll never be set up in time for the afternoon. Come dear, let's make haste.'

The Clydesdale's front hooves stamp the ground. Professor Moffat puts one boot on the step, ready to swing himself up on the cart before stopping.

'I might check the caravan one last time, in case we have forgotten something.'

'I have checked it.' Mrs Moffat looks straight ahead.

'Very well. Thanks, dear.' He reaches up to swing himself onto the box but stops again, scratching his head.

'It might be best to bring the actual letter of invitation along. I'll not be a minute.'

'I've got that, too. It's right here.' Mrs Moffat waves the paper and tucks it back into her coat.

'Very well. You do think of everything.' His face looks suddenly panicked. 'Oh, but I have completely forgotten to…'

'I'VE DONE IT,' hollers Mrs Moffat, and we nearly fall off the end of the cart, laughing. The Bruce's cage is attached by a rope, and Mr Robertson sits on its box, ready to pull the brake if we go downhill.

Our journey isn't fast, but it is merry enough, once we have covered some miles and Professor Moffat isn't tempted to run back for something.

I am impatient to see Balmoral Castle. I have heard so much about it, and when it finally comes into view behind a row of very fine trees, I am speechless. Can there be a handsomer residence in the whole of the Empire?

'It is most happily situated, is it not, my dear?' Merriweather Moffat speaks as if he was personally responsible for furnishing the Queen with such a house, and we all laugh once more.

We are expected. Two liveried gentlemen meet us at the gates and direct us towards the beautiful walled garden from which we can already hear laughing and lively conversation. Even though the day is cooler, the ladies are wearing gowns and shawls only—it really is a most pleasantly sheltered place. A young child is riding a small white pony on the lawn, bouncing and giggling each time the servant leads it into a trot.

'Over here, if you please.' The young man who directs us is one of the Royal party, lively and warm.

'That is Prince Henry of Battenberg, the Queen's son-in-law! Look at his moustache!' Ishie seems to know about so many illustrious personages. But her voice is strained. I raise my eyebrows. 'What is it?'

'Father says that I must not perform this afternoon after all, even if my ankle is better. He deems it too much of a risk, for I might fall again and displease the Queen. But I have bandaged it tightly, and it is certainly not broken.' She catches my eye and then looks away.

'It matters little,' she mumbles.

I'm not sure I believe her.

Mr Robertson assembles the stage, and the fit-up beside it. I prepare for the performance as I have done countless times before and memorise all the little alterations to the script one last time. The Queen's favourite colour. Royal names, woven into the story. The mention of kilts and plaids, for the Queen herself is said to adore the patterns of our heritage. I tie small bunches of blossoming heather to each side of the booth for a pretty effect.

And then she appears, upright and graceful, even though

she is old. I don't need to think about it: my body knows what to do and it bows all by itself. The Queen takes a seat under an elegant shelter and converses with her guests while we finish our preparations in hushed voices.

'We must not make a nuisance of ourselves, for a great honour has been bestowed upon us,' Professor Moffat whispers earnestly as we slot the last prop into place. A short time before we begin, Mrs Moffat takes him aside and speaks to him gently behind the puppet booth. I can't hear what they are saying, but I do see a smile exchanged, his hand placed gently on her shoulder, and then they emerge, ready for the conjuring act as soon as the Royal party gives the word.

But something unexpected is happening. The Queen has got up. Queen Victoria Regina herself is walking straight towards Ishie.

'We hope your ankle is much recovered, dear.' Queen Victoria says kindly. 'It was a most unfortunate incident. Do you still suffer?'

Ishie is almost frozen in a semi-curtsey. Her parents stand at a distance, no doubt struck by their daughter being so singled out.

'Yes, your Majesty,' she wheezes at last. 'Thank you; you are too kind. I think I am much improved.'

'We are glad to hear it. We should be delighted to see you dance once more, if your injury permits? You do move very prettily. Shall we see you dance today?'

The Queen is waiting, and I am sure she is accustomed to being answered without delay.

'May I, Father?' The plea in her voice would be sure to melt anyone's heart, and as a performer, Merriweather Moffat, of all people, should understand.

Mrs Moffat elbows her husband subtly in the side. 'If Your Majesty wishes it,' he nods. And if the occasion hadn't been so solemn, I'm sure Ishie would have flung her arms around her father's neck.

Queen Victoria turns to Merriweather Moffat: 'We are all in eager anticipation of your entertainment. You shall receive a written testimonial at the end, declaring our Royal approval. It may be of benefit in certain situations you may find yourself in. When shall you begin?'

'Directly, if Your Majesty wishes.' He bows almost with every word, and Mrs Moffat looks like she is biting back a laugh.

'We are delighted.' With this, the Queen turns and strides towards her seat, facing us. One or two whispered remarks from her are enough to silence the rest of the party who adjust their furniture, call over the children, settle the dogs and give us their whole attention. The Prince of Battenberg makes a witty remark, resulting in a restrained chuckle from the Queen, and I decide to focus on this man's open, smiling face, determined to favour everything, as I strike the first chord for Ishie.

She explodes into action, stepping, twirling, whirling and swirling, weaving her way from a slow, elegant piece to a frantic pace. She flips backwards, all the way off the little platform onto the grass where she tumbles forwards, backwards and even sideways. Professor Moffat plays the hard part of the melody while I accompany him with chords on my own fiddle. Ishie's tight bandage shows as she balances forward in an elegant Arabesque, but she cartwheels and spins into the final movements as if the accident had never happened. Back on the platform, she finishes with a double-somersault dismount which she has never done in public before, but lands surely, on both feet, her face already beaming before she has even straightened up, for she knows she has succeeded. The gasps at her risks turn to heartfelt applause, and the smiling Prince bellows "*Bravo*" in his German accent.

Mr Robertson's clowning is much appreciated, but the Royal Party respond with squeals of delight to our Punch and Judy opera, with particular fondness for our live Dog Toby who seems to know exactly how to behave in front of Royalty. We finish by forming a line and taking a bow together, and I take a deep breath. We did it!

A servant hands the Queen a sheet of paper. She writes a few lines and nods as the manservant leans over obligingly to dry the ink before sealing it.

He places the letter in Professor Moffat's hand. 'Her Majesty the Queen thanks you for your service and wishes you to accept the enclosed payment and reference. May it prove of some value to you.'

Professor Moffat opens the envelope only after we have left the castle behind us, some ten minutes into our journey back.

'Mark my words, friends,' he says, with difficulty, for he is overcome. 'This changes everything.'

CHAPTER 29

THE HIGHLAND AND THE LOWLAND WAYS

Both Mr Robertson and I have received a small bag of money for our trouble and I clutch the pouch to my chest. Too tired to cook on the camp fire, we retire to an inn to eat.

'If one cannot celebrate on a day like this, when *can* one celebrate?' Professor Moffat announces, raising a glass, and we all join him, clinking our glasses and wishing each other health and happiness. Until I see a leaflet, nailed up beside the bar.

Escaped prisoner believed to be hiding in Perthshire.

The likeness is unskilled this time, but a quick glance to my friend confirms, he has seen it too. Again and again, his eyes drift to the picture, and then to the reward sum beneath it.

We stay a while to avoid arousing suspicion, but Mr Robertson makes his excuses early and heads back to camp.

We find him there, by candlelight, leaning over a wide plank of wood into which he has fashioned holes for attaching to the side of the caravan.

'*Professor Moffat's Royal Entertainment Show*' it reads in swirly circus-lettering, without a single mistake; it looks as though he has outlined it first in pencil. A proper sign-maker could not have done this better.

'Think of it as a thank-ye from me, sir.' The men's handshake lasts a long time.

Nevertheless, I sleep fitfully that night, fancying every passing rider to be a sheriff officer.

The next day we pack up early. Even Mrs Moffat seems a little tense, keeping an eye on the road as we begin our slow journey south. According to the Moffats, the plan is to travel to Edinburgh along the coast, taking in the last of the seaside season's visitors. The Clydesdale struggles to pull the caravan *and* the bear in the cage, so we take many breaks and travel but a few miles each day.

Days turn into weeks. Toby grows. I feel my feet filling my father's boots and somehow, Mr Robertson does not look all that huge anymore. When we reach the Kingdom of Fife, I use my wages, carefully stowed away in the lining of my cap, to buy a collar for Toby. It's proper leather, and so much more well-to-do than the string.

What a place the Fife coast is! The sun shimmers on the Firth of Forth with diamond lines along each wave. We set up the puppet booth in the afternoon sun, ready to catch the change of shift. And out they come, boys much smaller than me, faces blackened and eyes strained by ten, sometimes eighteen hours underground. They stop and watch. Mr Robertson says that they will only get a few hours' rest before heading down into the pit once more, so I perform as well as I can for them. I feel very, very lucky.

When I walk around with the collecting hat afterwards, I skip the rows and rows of collier children, many younger than myself. How can I take from those who toil so much for so little? Father used to say: 'You can't help every creature in need, but you can pray, Phineas. You can pray.'

One small boy with eyes already dull with dust and darkness stands beside our sign, painted in glossy splendour: '*Professor Moffat's Royal Entertainment Show*'.

My world is a rainbow. His is a shadow.

He could be me, and I could be him, and life simply isn't fair. I do pray for him heartily that night.

We travel along the Fife coast and eventually cross on the ferry towards Edinburgh, the Moffats' base for the dark season. What a great city Auld Reekie is! So many steam trains coming and going, so many people travelling so many streets in so many carriages and carts. And, in the middle of it all, a hill: the magnificent Arthur's Seat.

Mr Robertson and I climb it on our very first weekend there. He points out the mighty Firth of Forth and the ferry on which we crossed, Duddingston village and the splendid harbour of Leith. I squint to make out the places across the water and marvel at Edinburgh Castle, seemingly hewn out of the volcanic rock on which it stands. Neither of us mention its cousin in Inverness.

The flat the Moffats have rented is near the Grassmarket: a ground floor entrance, with a yard and a small annex where Mr Robertson and I sleep. It feels almost unnatural to be stretching out on a mattress again, and hear the near-constant carts and carriages rattling down the Cowgate. We are not the only ones living in comfort: Professor Moffat has arranged for The Bruce to winter in a rich gentleman's private zoological menagerie, and Mr Robertson and I spend a very enjoyable afternoon there to see how our bear is settling into his generous enclosure.

The snow begins to fall almost as soon as we make our home here. There are fewer engagements now, but Mr Robertson makes himself useful by building a collapsible stage for next spring, with proper treads which fold away underneath. Professor Moffat keeps to his study, writing letters, placing advertisements in the papers and, above all, creating new and fresh scripts for our puppets. He even purchases a new character for our set: A Strong-Man, and I am amazed how battered and splintered our figures look in comparison to this shiny new one. It inspires me to try to restore our old puppets to their former splendour. I spend hours at the Moffats' kitchen table, with horsehair brushes made from the Clydesdale's tail and mane, and touch up every blemish. Even Punch with his hooked nose looks presentable again.

Through the windows, I spot flickering candles in fir trees, brought inside after the fashion of the late Prince Albert. It looks so very odd to me. I'm doubly surprised when I open the door to a snow-clad Professor Moffat one night before Christmas and he has brought just such a tree. A real, green, living tree.

'Phineas, would you be so kind as to fetch Mr Robertson, please? I would appreciate a helping hand.'

Even Mr Robertson groans and puffs, but the tree soon stands upright in the good front room, wedged into a bucket of wet sawdust and sand to keep it fresh.

'What is it?' Mr Robertson's forehead is so furrowed, I can't help laughing.

'It's a Christmas tree. Watch, gentlemen!'

'Christmas tree,' mutters Mr Robertson, shaking his head.

Merriweather Moffat reveals a small paper parcel and carefully unfolds it: inside is a strange collection of metal clips. 'Like this!' he announces as if he had invented the custom himself. 'Clip it on, Phineas, so the round part faces upward.'

Ah, I see how it is meant to work. I fix my first clip on.

'Very good—now, distribute them evenly, that's right. Do you see, Mr Robertson? Alice, don't you love it?'

Mrs Moffat stands in the corner of the room, clutching a pack of wax candles. 'I do love it, dear. Who would not?'

'Then place the candles in! No time like the present!' Professor Moffat's cheeks glow with excitement.

The street lamps outside are lit by the time we finish. Merriweather Moffat strikes a match and lights the first candle.

I am not sure what I expected. But maybe not the pleasant scent of a woodland, right in our home. The light of thirty candles, dancing and reflecting in the windowpane, casting ever-changing shadows against the wall, the furniture, and our faces, too.

'Extinguish the candles now, Alice,' Professor Moffat says suddenly, for all of us have sunk into an awed silence. 'We must save on the wax. We will light it on Christmas Eve. They say the Queen knows how to make merry at Christmas, and after a year like ours, so shall we!' He reaches into his coat and brandishes a book.

'What's that?' Mr Robertson asks again. He is wary of books.

'It's a story. A ghost story called *A Christmas Carol*, by Mr Charles Dickens. And those of us who can read, shall read it to the others at night. And on Christmas, we will go to church, and we shall have a goose! Isn't that right dear?'

Mrs Moffat nods and looks at him in a way that makes me happy and sad at the same time. Did my parents ever have love like this between them? Is this what my sister, Lizzie, ran away to find? And did she find it?

I receive my first ever Christmas present. When my parents were alive, I might get a small present at Hogmanay, but never at Christmas. All these new ways. They are not the Highland ways.

But I find that I bear them very cheerfully.

Chapter 30

MORNINGSIDE

With the caravan stored in Silverknowes and the Clydesdale returned to the stables it was hired from, we earn our daily bread by wheeling the booth to church bazaars, markets and private house parties. The advertisement Professor Moffat has placed in the Scotsman newspaper keeps us busy enough.

Whenever I see a "*WANTED*" poster for Mr Robertson, I tear it down when I know no-one is looking. I block the wooden stairs from my mind, the giant's fist and the whisky reek. I resolve to be happy with my new life, for I am blessed! From time to time, from the corner of my eye, I fancy I see him: Uncle Ewan, passing in the street, lurking outside St Giles, patrolling George IV Bridge. But I can never be sure. Fear is a curse.

'Morning, Phineas.'

Mrs Moffat takes the fresh bread from my hand—I am the earliest riser, and Toby and I usually make the trip to the baker.

'The two of you need to set off in good time today. A church bazaar along the Morningside Road. It's a fair walk with all our things.'

I nod. The church committee have asked for an early start, and for several performances throughout the day. Ishie and Mrs Moffat are meeting friends, Mr Robertson has a day off and Professor Moffat is already loading our pull-along cart up in the street.

I wolf down a slice of bread with butter and run out to join him.

'Phineas! How is your voice today?'

My voice has become temperamental all of a sudden. I suppose it had to break eventually. 'I feel well enough. Do I sound right?' I answer in puppet Judy's high voice, and even though there is a little crack, Merriweather Moffat laughs.

'Let's not dither.'

'Have you had breakfast, Professor Moffat, sir?'

He looks at me with a vacant look before working out the answer to my question from somewhere in his crowded mind.

'I have not!' He spreads his hands out in a 'wait' gesture and bustles through the open door into the flat. It can't be more than thirty seconds before he reappears, crumbs on his waistcoat and the remnant of a slice of bread disappearing into his mouth. I run through the lane to the back yard to the water closet, rinse my hands in the trough and then we are ready. Hauling the cart up Candlemaker Row and past Greyfriars Church is the hardest work. We make our way past the expanse of the Meadows before dipping down the hill to Morningside.

Professor Moffat checks his pocket watch every few minutes, but we arrive in plenty of time and set up in a quiet side room. It doesn't take long before people begin to file in. Ladies with handbags and frosty coats, gentlemen with briefcases and a minister with a long robe and a ready smile. This is not how I remember church at all, with bright colours and noise and happiness. The bazaar serves to raise funds for the building, and for some missionary in Africa. For us it means a certain income, and the audience is very pleasant and genteel today. I keep Toby on a lead through a back door until the audience has swelled to such a size that it's worth starting, and the prim lady who is our contact gives us the nod. Before I pull the curtain open, I peek through for a final check, as I do every time, although I know very well that Uncle Ewan is not likely to appear in a church hall in Morningside, to watch a Punch and Judy opera.

My voice holds reasonably well throughout the many performances of the day, only sliding out of control during the last fight with the Policeman, but it is easily covered up. By now, Professor Moffat and I can anticipate exactly what the other will do and say. The audience laugh and scream, and we draw on their energy. Through the small flap at the side of the fit-up, I catch sight of a small boy, no more than three and with a good head of dark hair.

The little boy clutches the skirt of the lady beside him, probably his mother. For some reason, I can't take my eyes off him.

Professor Moffat kicks me in the shin. Oh Lord, I've missed my cue. I don't allow myself the luxury of checking on the sweet wee boy again. *Focus, Phineas!*

The applause at the end of the show is magnified by the walls of the compact hall. I squeeze out of the back of the booth, join Merriweather Moffat in bowing and pass the collecting hat round, beginning at the back so people won't have a chance to slip out through the door before donating something to the church roof fund.

It is the biggest audience of the day, and as my eyes travel over the faces, I make out the small boy again, right at the back now. His mother, a pretty young woman, is talking to an elderly lady by the door, but even though her face is turned sideways, I am suddenly electrified. She reminds me of…

No, it isn't her.

It definitely isn't.

Father said she was dead to him, in disgrace. He said she was sure to end up in a workhouse.

She would definitely not be frequenting well-to-do

church bazaars in Morningside, would she?

The woman turns, as if to look straight at me, and I don't know why, but I lower my head immediately. Anyone who shows too much interest in me is a threat. I'm on the run after all. I drop to my knees and attend to all the small children at the front who want to stroke Toby after his starring performance. The next time I raise my head and peek out from under the rim of my cap, she is gone.

It's dark by the time we head off with our cart, and I wheel it up Morningside hill on my own, for Professor Moffat has run into an old friend at the bazaar and wanted to stop for a pint of ale before catching me up.

The cobbled streets are emptying. No-one likes to travel on winter roads at night, and it seems that in this respect, the Highland and the Lowland ways are the same. There are men spilling out from public houses onto the road, and in the distance, I watch the lights in the church go out. There is a little snow in the air, intermittent sparks of white, catching the light from the street lamps. I draw my collar up, pull the cap deep into my face and heave the heavy cart onwards.

Until I hear steps behind me.

I speed up and listen at the same time. I am a wanted boy, after all.

They become urgent steps.

And now they are running steps.

My legs feel very, very heavy all of a sudden.

For whoever it is behind me, he will be upon me in a second.

CHAPTER 31

ALIVE AND WELL

'Ex... excuse me?'

I nearly drop the long pulling handle of our puppet cart. In front of me stands the woman I was looking at earlier; I am sure of it. She does not have her boy with her now, her hat is askew and there is snow in her hair. Her cheeks are flushed with the exercise.

She looks at me and says nothing, searching my features for something. I do the same. Her face falls.

'I'm... I'm sorry. I thought you were someone else.' She backs away slowly and my voice falters properly as I croak: 'Lizzie?'

Before I have finished speaking, I am swept into a tight, tight embrace. I have not been embraced since before my Mother passed from this world into the next. Miss Garrow put her hand around my shoulder, awkward and clammy, on the night of my father's death, but never again.

This young woman, so respectable-looking and pretty, does not let me go, but kisses my forehead and cheeks.

'Phineas! Phineas, I never thought…' Her face is wet, and I'm not ashamed to own it, so is mine. 'I thought it sounded a little like you, but I never thought… how…what are you doing here? And how are Mother and Father?'

She steps back and looks at me properly. 'I've thought of you all every day, all those years. How come…'

And something filters into her eyes: the realisation that the son of a strict Highland Reverend would never be a travelling showman, if all was well.

The snow falls thicker now, and I pull the cart under a ledge to shelter us from the worst. I tell before I ask, which surely is the worst of manners, but I can't help it. My shoulders shiver, and she winces when I speak of the influenza that claimed our mother, and the vile confrontation with Finlayson that took our father. She listens intently, stretching her hand out to rub my arm whenever I shudder too much. She gasps properly when I tell her about being forced to move into the butcher's house. Mr Finlayson's offer was considered such a gesture of benevolence then—he wouldn't allow the unfortunate boy to face the poorhouse. I end by confessing that everybody in Inverness believes I set the market on fire.

'And you've been travelling with strangers ever since?'

'Not strangers, no!' I laugh for the first time in the half-hour that we have been standing here, in the snow.

'Where are you staying?'

'Grassmarket. But what about you, Lizzie? What

happened? Mother cried and cried, and Father never...'

'Never spoke of me again. I know.' She looks uncomfortable. 'I ran away with a young gentleman, a travelling student. It's a long story.' She brightens again. 'We live down there now, in Comiston Road. My husband William, me and little Archie—you might have seen him earlier. I took Archie home after the bazaar, but I couldn't settle. Even though I declared it impossible, I had to come back. I had to know for certain that it wasn't you.'

She laughs through her tears. 'But Lord, my hair!' She sweeps it to the side, tucking it back into the bun beneath her hat as best as she can. 'Can you come tomorrow, Phineas? After church, I mean? Here is my card with the address.'

Will she judge me when she hears that I have no social engagements at all, apart from our performances? That the life of people like the Moffats is spontaneous and free, and altogether more joyful than I could have ever imagined?

'Yes, of course I'll come. So you are...'

'Married? Yes.' She raises her left hand and reveals a wedding ring.

Married. None of this matches the tale of disgrace and ruin told in Inverness.

'I'll explain it all tomorrow,' she laughs, 'if you've not caught too much of a chill by then!' She gives my shoulder a last rub. 'Two o'clock? You can take luncheon with us!' And with that she turns and walks away. Just as I hoist the heavy handle up onto my shoulder again, I see her turn and wave. I raise my hand in return and walk a few paces up the hill, turn and wave again and then pick up my speed.

My sister, alive and well. The clean smell of her hair, the velvet collar of her coat, the fresh smile and the eyes so like my own, grey and blue with a fleck of brown to one side. All those years, I was alone in the world.

Now I have friends, and a sister again.

'I'm coming wi' ye! Don't try tae tell me otherwise.'

'But Mr Robertson, I'll be perfectly fine.'

'I'm the reason ye're this far from home. Taking trip across town all by yerself, not knowing where ye're going! I willnae hear of it! I'm coming.' Mr Robertson sits opposite me in the tiny annex, cross-legged on his narrow bed, and I wonder whether his prison cell was any bigger than this.

'I do know where to go. I'll be safe.'

'Look, Phineas! I'll come and that's final! I'll watch ye safely in, and I'll wait somewhere nearby.' He glares across at me and I wonder if I can read something into that look: Worry? Hope? Fear?

Ten minutes later we are on our way. The journey takes next to no time at all, considering last time I was pulling a cart with a whole puppet fit-up and case on it. The low winter sun casts a hazy light onto the frozen grass of Bruntsfield Links, and we march down the hill, past gentlemen and ladies in their Sunday best, spilling out of church doors and shaking ministers' hands. Heading home to eat their roasts no doubt.

I pick up my pace, suddenly uncomfortable in my threadbare breeches, a little on the short side, and my scuffed boots.

Mr Robertson has traded a hand-carved set of finger puppets he made for a long woollen coat, and he does look almost like a gentleman today. I relax a little.

At the bottom of the hill, Comiston Road is straight ahead. I check the card and point. 'That's the one, there. The black door.'

'On ye go. I'll wait.'

A mid-terrace town house. My sister must either be a live-in-servant (though she did not look like one) or there has been terrible misunderstanding. This is not the house of someone disgraced, even if she is married now. With reluctance, I lift the knocker and let it fall against the brass doorplate. Furtive steps on the other side, and a kind-faced elderly woman in simple Sunday attire opens the door. 'Young Master Phineas? Mr Sinclair and Mrs Sinclair are expecting you.'

I am led through the hall where the old woman offers to take my cap and jacket, and then shows me into a grand reception room. The big bay window faces out to the street. I do hope Mr Robertson finds a sheltered space to wait.

An ornately plastered archway leads into a dining room where a tall, smiling man in a frock coat walks towards me. 'You must be Phineas. Yes, I can certainly see the likeness. Elizabeth has often spoken of you. But where are my manners! My name is William Sinclair. I'm delighted to make your acquaintance.'

The door flies open and Archie runs in, followed by Lizzie who looks simply lovely, all dressed in blue. I still can't fathom how it could all be possible.

'Phineas! You found it!'

We sit down to luncheon and Archie is scolded for not eating his greens. After living on bread, cheese and stew for months, I have to remind myself to chew thirty times before swallowing. I mustn't show Lizzie up.

At last, my sister can speak plainly. 'Phineas, Mother and Father disapproved of my match with my husband. He was travelling through Inverness as a student, and we met at the guesthouse where I was working. Father was strict about these things. I am not proud of it, but one night, I climbed out through the dining room window of the manse and left. I should never have done so, had I known what you were going to face…' Her voice cracks and she looks up at the ceiling.

'You didn't know. Please don't worry.'

'We got married as soon as we got to Edinburgh. At first, we stayed in the old town, but when William passed his law exams, we moved here. He is a partner in a firm on George Street.'

Her eyes glow with pride, and William Sinclair smiles an easy smile.

'At first I wrote, but my letters were returned to me unopened. Father... I wish I had had a chance to ...'

Her voice falters once more, and William sitting beside her strokes her back.

'But anyway, we are comfortable, and we are in a position to make you so, too. I have spoken to William about all you have said to me.' She pauses and looks uncertainly at her husband. 'We both think that you need to go back to Inverness to make a statement, before Ewan Finlayson can do more harm.'

'He should be charged with manslaughter,' William Sinclair nods.

'And your name can be cleared,' Lizzie adds.

I'm beginning to think that maybe the duck is not as tasty as I first thought it was.

'I can't.' I finally force my lips to release the words when all of us are disturbed by a commotion outside. Screaming, running feet, shouts of 'Police' and 'I saw him first'.

I fling back my chair and run to the window.

'Mr Robertson!' I whisper before pelting through the hall, grabbing my jacket and cap and hurtling out into the cold afternoon air.

CHAPTER 32

BOUNTY HUNTERS

'It's definitely him!' shouts a young man on the corner of the street. 'The wanted man. He's hiding in the lane between those buildings.'

Mr Robertson must have heard, for he shoots out through the gap, runs towards me, thinks better of it and hooks right round, back into the busy crowd on Morningside Road. I run after him as best as I can, though his strides are long. About five or six men are running alongside me. No doubt each of them is after a portion of the reward.

'Don't let him get away!' I yell. 'I saw him!' I point left, even though I glimpsed Mr Robertson duck behind a parked carriage and sneak into a lane on the right.

To my astonishment, all the men follow me and we thunder down the road in the opposite direction until we are out of breath. 'Where is he? Is he armed, do you think?' a portly man pants.

I try to answer, but he ignores me and turns to the young man. 'Could be anywhere behind these buildings.'

Even now, I do not tell an outright lie; my conscience won't let me. Instead, I focus my gaze on a random outhouse, way down the street on the left, and narrow my eyes, walking forward very slowly.

The rest of the men pick up my cue and take an interest. 'In there, is he?' the older man asks. I shrug. He reaches for a broken plank of wood lying in a lane and steps forward.

'Sir; I recognised him first,' protests another young man.

'Let's force him out between us and share the reward,' a third suggests.

I draw back, slowly, very slowly, but I needn't have worried—they hardly even noticed I was there. Merely a boy, not worth worrying about.

They advance in a ring towards the empty outhouse. I do not stick around long enough to see what they'll do once they realise.

When I arrive back at the flat in the Grassmarket, Mrs Moffat is already halfway through shaving Mr Robertson's beard off. A thick paste of ground coffee beans covers his usual sandy-coloured hair and eyebrows.

'You need to lie low for a while,' she advises, 'but if anyone catches a glimpse of you they will be hard-pushed to recognise you now. I'll go out directly to my cousin in Leith. He is your build, or thereabouts, and he may well have some clothes you can borrow. Leave the paste in for an hour, that way it will last a while, I've been told. And once my husband and daughter return from their visit, we'll make plans.'

She sets off alone.

'Thank ye, Phin,' Mr Robertson mumbles, as low as can be. I shrug.

'Don't mention it. I'll brew some tea.' It gives me something to do, fetching water from the tap outside and placing the kettle on the range. It builds up to a low whistle when my world is shaken by the smallest of sounds.

A knock on the front door.

Mr Robertson and I stare each other. What do we do?

I recover first. 'Out?' I mouth, pointing to the yard, but he shakes his head and he's right—tenements from four sides overlook the yard, and with the coffee paste still in his hair, he can't be seen.

He points to the press and I wonder whether such a tall man could fit into the cupboard at all, but somehow, he does.

The knocking has become loud and urgent. 'We know you're in there! Open the door if you know what's good for you!'

Of course, the whole dwelling house will be searched. They will find my friend, and then our cover will be blown. He will be locked up forever, or worse—hanged. I will be returned to Ewan Finlayson.

It is striking, how much the brain can process in a few

seconds. I fear the door will be beaten down. I brace myself and unbar it, turning the handle slowly with Toby growling at my feet.

'Mr Sinclair? What are you doing here?' I am so astonished that my voice jumps into puppet mode. Lizzie is behind him, but no police. No one else.

'Phineas, we can help you. Elizabeth told me all about your plight.' The lawyer looks over his shoulder where people are passing in the street.

'May we come in?'

I throw the door wide. They file into the narrow hallway without giving away how unlike their own house this is. There is no judgement in their eyes either.

'Where is your friend Robertson?'

He may be Lizzie's husband, but how can I trust him with the concerns of another? I shake my head, but Lizzie takes my hand.

'Please, Phineas. William is a lawyer. A good lawyer, and a partner in a firm already. If anyone can fight your corner in a court of law, it is him. And he wants to do it.' Lizzie's eyes plead and suddenly I feel tired. So very, very tired of being grown up and of hiding and of pretending, and of managing alone. I sway slightly. In any case, Toby is sniffing at the gap at the bottom of the press where Mr Robertson is hiding. I feel too tired to do anything about that either.

'There is a strange smell in here,' Lizzie observes in the

silence. The answer comes in the form of Mr Robertson, as the door to the press creaks open, 'Ye're looking fer me, I believe,' he states, his voice dripping with defeat. 'Leave the boy alone. He hasnae done anything wrong.'

Mr Sinclair takes a step towards him, and I half-imagine handcuffs or some other form of restraint or trickery, but no—Mr Sinclair is only offering my friend his hand to shake.

'William Sinclair. A pleasure to meet you. My young brother-in-law speaks fondly of you.'

Mr Robertson is so surprised, he shakes the hand back.

'Now, before I say anything else, let me assure you that I am on your side. And I am certain that I can help, too. There are still several gaps in the boy's narrative, but if you'd do me the honour of answering my questions truthfully, it would be a privilege to advise you on the best course to take. Now, Phineas—would you be so kind as to pour us some tea?'

My legs barely hold up, and once I have seen to the guests, I sink onto a chair in the kitchen and let the words wash over me. '*Returned soldier... found my betrothed married to someone else... altercation... wrongful accusation... assault... prison... fugitive... kidnapper... in hiding...*' My head sinks down onto my chest, I feel my sister's gentle hand on my shoulder, and soon I hear nothing at all anymore.

CHAPTER 33

THE RETURN

Three months later, I clutch Toby close to my chest as the steam blows past the train window, hiding Perth from view as we leave, and I think of The Bruce, now permanently settled at the menagerie, and with a female bear companion too. Professor Moffat made a loss with the sale, of course, but 'a principled man must be granted leave to change his mind,' he said, insisting he owed the bear this kindness. Across from me, Mr Robertson leans back in extremely respectable-looking clothes, borrowed from my sister's husband. William himself sits beside him, reading a legal book and taking notes while the Moffats complete my row. It was decided Lizzie should stay in Edinburgh with Archie to protect the wee lad from any unrest. And unrest is bound to follow, once we have done what we have come to do. I run over the plan, again and again, but how can we possibly succeed? It's hare-brained!

A whirlpool of worries begins to swirl in my mind, but Mrs Moffatt distracts me by offering me a cold meat pie.

The majestic Cairngorms glisten in the sun and the sky is so blue that I can barely believe this is Scotland at all. Still, there is a shiver in the air as we slow down. Passengers shuffle past to disembark in Aviemore and I begin to steel myself for seeing it all again.

The ruined market, directly opposite the station, surely still smouldering after all this time.

'Dinnae worry, Phineas. Nobody will recognise ye looking like that.' Mr Robertson brushes my hair aside with his fingers and I lean forward to whisper to him. 'What if he's there? Will the plan work then?'

'The plan will work, whether he comes or not. You just need to stick tae it. Believe in it!' With that he sits back again and lets his eyes skip over the ever-changing landscape. The distillery has flown by on the left. Not long now.

My heart begins to beat very fast as the train horn blows and a new cloud of steam obscures my view. Toby licks my hand, as if he knows the fear that is welling up inside me.

The line ends here in Inverness. All passengers in the three wooden carriages reach up to retrieve their luggage from the high racks and shuffle towards the exits. Porters appear to help the more well-to-do with their cases, but are forced to wait until the middle classes have alighted. I remain seated, motionless.

'Mr Robertson; shall we?' Professor Moffat stretches. Of course, the fit-up is in the goods compartment. It takes a while to manoeuvre it through the doors and onto the platform, but finally, here we stand, Mr Robertson and I, side by side on a train platform in Inverness. Hiding behind starched collars and under top hats, and hoping to fool the whole town in which we both grew up.

'I have a bad feeling about this,' I mutter to Mr Robertson as I help him pull the cart towards the exit. And then I see it.

Even though I expected it, it still takes my breath away. The façade of the market still stands: the larger triple-arch of the entrance, flanked by the two smaller arches. The balustrade along the top is charred and dirty. It looks like work is going on behind, as if a new roof was being constructed, but nothing is as it was. A great sadness floods through me.

'Phineas!' Mr Robertson elbows me so hard that I almost drop Toby's lead.

'Dinnae look now, but that woman yonder has not taken her eyes off you since you stepped out into the street. Does she look familiar?'

I bend down to stroke Toby and peek up through my hair, so carefully parted before, but now hanging like a curtain in front of my eyes. A flash of ice cuts through my heart, and I can barely straighten up again. Because, rushing along the street towards the bridge and looking at me again over her shoulder, is Miss Garrow.

CHAPTER 34

THE SHOWDOWN

'Uncle Ewan's housekeeper!' I breathe to Mr Robertson. *She has gone to fetch him, and he will know that I'm here. He will know.*

Professor Moffat nods heavily. 'We must hurry then. Begin before he arrives.' We quicken our step and head for the Exchange Square in front of the Town House where all sorts of traders are already selling their wares. We have booked a sheltered corner under an archway, making sure our voices can echo over the surrounding noise. I'm wound tight like a spring, but even now I can appreciate that Professor Moffat has done well, securing the coveted entertainment space at the Victoria Day Fair and making sure that the whole town will be here to watch. We assemble the puppet fit-up with practised hands, but my heart is not in it. Ah, Mrs Smith from down the road crosses the square behind me, but doesn't even give me a second glance. There's Martin Bell I went to the Raining's school with, but he's manning a stand with vegetables. Self-consciously, I allow my hair to flop down in front of my forehead, but I don't feel completely safe until I'm hidden away in the booth. Arranging the puppets and setting everything up in the right place allows me to pretend I'm not here at all. It's only another performance. Another day we earn our bread. It could be anywhere.

I can't resist opening the curtain a chink and peeking through: a sea of faces. Not only the children, some of whom I remember—no, many, many adults are also partial to a spot of Punch. The plan could work. It really could work.

Professor Moffat appears beside me in the booth, secures the swazzle into the roof of his mouth and nods. He gives the signal through the back of the booth and Mrs Moffat steps forward.

'Ladies and gentlemen, children and …others.'

This raises a laugh.

'*Professor Moffat's Royal Entertainment* presents you with a Punch and Judy Opera…'

There are a few claps and cheers.

'With a difference,' she continues. 'We all know what a villain Punch is. But could there be another villain, as treacherous as he? Welcome to a brand-new show, never performed before and written especially for this honoured audience of Inverness.'

She strikes up the first chord on her accordion. I almost

pity these people: they are expecting a cheerful tale, but we must give them something else.

My Judy-hand flies up and I begin, forgetting all that lies on the other side of this flimsy cloth. I will not peek. If Ewan Finlayson is there, my courage will falter for certain.

'Punch! Where are you, you scoundrel, you wastrel, you fool!' echoes my high-pitched voice. 'Give me the baby!'

There are giggles from the children all throughout the first chase, a gasp when Punch throws the Baby into the audience and deadly silence when Punch waits for the Policeman to come. But he is not coming. Punch gets impatient. 'Call with me, children. He must be terribly busy.' The audience roar, until finally, my Policeman puppet appears. 'What are you all making this racket for?' I demand in my lowest voice and Professor Moffat whispers "*louder*" into my ear. The next part I bellow out so loudly that I give myself a fright. 'I was busy questioning young MacLennan, the night guard of the market that burnt down last June. Would you believe: HE FELL and damaged the gas pipe that set the market on fire. Far from being responsible for that fire, the runaway boy Phineas pulled him from the burning wreckage and saved his life! Saved his life! MacLennan blamed the boy, you see. And you call me away to deal with Punch? I was taking a confession! You'd better have a very good reason.'

It's just as well that I can't see the audience. The laughter sounds more half-hearted and confused, but who would blame them?

The usual chase begins, to giggles and laughter from the children, though I can hear adult voices murmur, too. When we have completed the first chase, the two puppets hang over the edge of the stage, both supposedly puffed out and out of breath. Now for part two of the revelation.

'Do you honestly think you are the most despicable villain in the land Punch?' my Policeman puppet bellows.

'I know so. I killed Judy and the Baby,' comes the answer from Professor Moffat's puppet.

'Well I wouldn't be so sure. Do you remember the day when...'

There is a commotion in the audience. I peek through the side gap before I remember that I wasn't going to, and I see him, right at the back: Uncle Ewan. He has brought two—no three—policemen with him.

The audience continues to mutter.

'The day when...' I raise my voice. 'When the desperate Reverend Ephraim MacFadden visited the butcher Finlayson to plead for a loan, so his wife could see a doctor? That was the night she died. Do you know that the BUTCHER (I yell every word now. Everyone must hear!) punched the Reverend in anger and pushed him down the stairs in a violent struggle? And the next thing he did was to pour half a bottle of whisky down the dying man's throat to hide his own guilt. Finlayson branded the man of God a drunkard! And do you know that he took in the Reverend's son Phineas, who saw it all, so that he could beat him and threaten him and feed him lies?'

'Enough. Move on,' whispers Moffat in my ear and I nod. The audience are unsettled, and I sense some sort of movement towards the booth, but I continue, nodding the puppet's head vigorously.

'So, Punch; it's real villains like Ewan Finlayson who should be dealt with. Every word of what I have told you is true. But now, I'm going to catch you and throw you into prison!' The accordion music picks up again as we run our next chase, with children laughing, while the adults in the audience mutter more loudly. I wonder if MacLennan is there too.

I will keep going, until the show is done, or until I am physically dragged from the booth. More chases, until the Devil makes his final speech, and my voice cracks as I deliver it. I make up for it in volume. 'I'm taking you Punch, and there shall be no rescue for you. But, MacLennan, liar, and Ewan Finlayson, murderer—make no mistake—justice will come to you too!'

I am dripping in sweat as I drag the Punch puppet down. The booth is shaking, and I can see hands reaching in through the performance window.

I'd know those hands anywhere.

Merriweather Moffat stumbles sideways into me with the crowd pressing in, and there is no applause at all. Something splinters and I crouch low, pull out of the booth backwards and wriggle out through the crowd. A million arms and legs are trying to get to the booth. Will Merriweather Moffat be all right?

I need to get to the Sheriff Court, and quickly. I can scarcely believe that we have even made it this far. The Exchange Square is in uproar. I keep running, just as I did that night. Heavy footsteps fall very close behind me, and despite myself, I look over my shoulder.

It's him.

Oh Lord, it's him!

There are others, following—trying to restrain him— but Uncle Ewan pushes them away roughly and lumbers after me with gigantic strides, gaining on me with every step. Closer and closer; I can hear his rasping breath. He is tall, his legs are long and he is built like an Angus bull. Approaching the Sherriff Court, I hook right to throw my pursuer off balance. It seems to work. This time, I make straight for the front door. There is a guard, but I suspect his job is to keep people in, not out. I don't stop to ask. The stone floor thuds cold, and there is a sudden silence once the door closes behind me. Has William Sinclair kept to his part of the plan?

He has—I can hear his voice through a door down the

corridor. Without waiting for permission, I follow it, but turn to see when I hear a struggle at the main door. A guard holds on to Uncle Ewan's wrist, another three surround him, but he is struggling like Samson against the Philistines, roaring his anger like a wounded stag.

The door before me opens and my brother-in-law and an old-looking man appear. 'There you are, Phineas. Now, sir, this is the young gentleman who witnessed the death, and the subsequent attempt to pervert the course of justice. Phineas, this officer is ready to take your official statement. Tell him exactly what happened. Truthfully.'

The commotion outside dies down as Uncle Ewan is led away for questioning. I breathe deeply.

'Nothing to worry about now,' Sinclair nods. 'Tell your story.'

I try to keep focused, but it has been such a long day. Still, everything depends on this statement, and I do my best. My brother-in-law seems pleased when I finish. The old man bids me sign the statement, but looks up at both of us uncertainly.

'The statement will be considered, I can promise you that. But if it's the word of a respectable citizen against the word of a child...'

'I'm thirteen,' I protest, but he shakes his head.

'You understand that a court of law is unlikely to convict the man, don't you? Without an...'

'An adult witness?'

I jump out of my seat at the voice at the door, sharp and rigid; it cuts right into my head. Now I am there again, at the foot of the stairs, hiding behind the hat stand rather than attending my dying father. And every day after, scolded again and again, by this voice. Miss Garrow's voice.

'Well, you have one. The boy tells the truth and I should have said so much sooner.' Prim and upright, she lowers herself onto the seat opposite the officer who sighs and turns over the page.

'Looks like I am going to have to take another statement.'

Mr Sinclair pats me on the shoulder as if to say *"how brave you've been"*, and I listen to Miss Garrow recount the tale, just as I saw it. She wipes away a tear at the whisky part, but otherwise her face is unmoved. She does not look at me.

The official scratches his head. 'There may be charges levelled at you too, Miss. On the grounds of aiding and abetting.'

'I understand,' Miss Garrow whispers. 'But for once; for ONCE, I am going to do what's right. We do terrible things out of fear.'

And at that point she does look at me. The fear in her eyes is the same fear that sent my stomach plummeting every morning I woke under Ewan Finlayson's roof. For the first time in all these years, I understand. And I give her the ghost of a grateful smile.

When William Sinclair and I step out of the building, the evening is drawing in, and an orange glow hangs over the hills to the west.

'You did it Phineas—and only you could have done. I'll send word to Elizabeth with the night post. She'll be worried sick about you.' Surprise jolts into his voice. 'But Mr Robertson, what are you doing here?'

We have turned the corner of the building and there he stands, staring up at the tree where we had our first encounter.

'Mr Robertson! If anyone recognises you…' I try to move him away by the elbow, but he stands rooted to the spot like the tree beside him, a strange look in his eyes. I try again.

'We agreed you wouldn't go near the court!'

William Sinclair cocks his head sideways, as if slowly understanding. 'You're not going to run anymore, are you?'

Mr Robertson shakes his head so faintly that I barely notice it. His eyes flit over to the entrance of the Sherriff Court; the same prison he escaped so many months ago.

'What are you going to do?' I whisper. My throat is dry, because I think I already know the answer.

'I'm going tae hand myself in.'

CHAPTER 35

INVERNESS, 1891: A NEW MARKET

All of us wait outside the prison this time: The Moffats, Ishie, Lizzie, little Archie and Mr Sinclair—and Mr Robertson—who was released after he stood trial and paid the fine in full, no more than three months after turning himself in. Thanks to Mr Sinclair's defence, the attempted murder charge was dropped (it turned out that his accuser, the only witness, was very unreliable). Mr Robertson was found guilty of only a breach of the peace. Mr Sinclair explained it all at the time, something about 'mitigating circumstances' and having been described as a 'man of excellent character' by the major of his former regiment, which supposedly made a difference.

We're all here. The sun is shining.

And out she comes.

I hardly recognise this Miss Garrow—she wears the plainest of skirts with no apron and no jacket. Her head is downcast.

'Go on.' Ishie nudges me and I step forward with the

flowers I brought.

'Miss Garrow.'

Her head jerks up and she flinches as if were holding a knife.

A pause. 'Phineas?'

And then she looks at the bunch of flowers in my hand.

Little by little, understanding travels to her watery eyes. She takes a hesitant step towards me.

I step forward too, and Miss Garrow does something she has not done in all the years we lived under the same roof.

She cries, properly cries.

Down in the town, people flood through the gates into the brand-new market building. There is a cacophony of noise outside: bagpipes, choirs, fiddlers and brass bands, so I'm glad we are performing at the Church Street end. We pull our cart through the new corridors with difficulty. I wave at everyone I recognise: neighbours, school friends from the Raining's school and market traders and they greet me back without suspicion—Young MacLennan admitted it all. Someone said he even sold his story to a newspaper, and because it was an accident, he wasn't deemed a criminal after all. In fact, I think I see his tall gangly figure at the very back of the crowd.

More and more children arrive. They sit on sacks, on the wall, on their fathers' shoulders and on the ground. At the front, there is a boy with boots much too big for him and a shiver of memory travels down my spine before I remember that all is well. My father's boots are scuffed and scratched now, and holes are opening along the seam. I'll need to replace them soon, and thanks to my wages from the Moffats, I can. All is well indeed.

The audience clap along with the rhythm of Ishie's dance. She bows. The accordion strikes up out front, and with a glance, Professor Moffat and I are ready. We don't need words anymore. I can't help laughing along with the audience as Mr Punch lands his first blow and our puppet movements weave in and out of each other like bobbins in a tapestry of colour and sound.

Before we catch the steam train back to Edinburgh in the late afternoon, Mr Robertson and I have another errand. We head out on the river path where we sneaked along that night so many months ago. Soon the little row of houses comes into view. We stop at the last one, whitewashed and low.

'Nae washing on the line this time,' he mumbles. 'Nae wonder. Cannae trust people no tae steal it.'

He smooths the parcel out, and I try to picture the moment when the front door will open and the man inside finds the brand-new pressed trousers, the expensive linen shirt and a carefully written card of apology. Written by me as to disguise the hand, and my spelling is better in any case. We place it on the step and swiftly walk back towards the town before we are seen.

'I can breathe better now,' Mr Robertson says, looking straight ahead. 'Dinnae feel a thief anymore.'

I nudge him and he laughs and I laugh harder, and before we know it, we're both running, chasing each other down towards the town until we're back below the castle and both of us puffing and out of breath.

THE END

Author's Note

Punch has been a labour of love. My love of puppetry, my love of all things Victorian—and my love of Scotland.

It's easy to cast my mind back to nine-year-old me, opening my Christmas parcel from my parents. In it was a Pelham Muffin-the-Mule marionette, and the first string puppet in an ever-expanding collection. If I close my eyes, I can still sense the smooth wood, the beautiful dappled paint effect, the magical way in which the tiniest pull on a string could make this creature move. No, better than that: make it come alive. Almost thirty years later, I was a puppeteer. My mule has been restrung and repaired many times over, but it is still the most treasured character in my collection.

So what could be more natural than to feature puppetry in my historical fiction? As a children's author, I had always been interested in the Victorian period, and couldn't help noticing that most children's books on the subject were set in London and focused heavily on the poorhouses, the factories of the industrial revolution and gruelling child labour. But was that the whole story? And where did Scotland fit in?

I began to read: Highland history, Queen Victoria's Balmoral diaries, newspaper articles about Victorian settings—and found exactly what I was looking for: a hook.

If at all possible, I like to root my historical fiction in real events. Having a direct link to reality helps me enormously, and a BBC article on the historical fire which destroyed the original Inverness Victorian Market was just what I needed for my novel's setting. Summer 1889 it was! The event now forms the opening chapters of PUNCH. The what-if questions quickly generated the backbone of the plot: what if a young boy was in the wrong place at the wrong time? What if the blame for the event was pinned on him? What if he found refuge with a section of society rarely portrayed, such as a travelling showman and his family? All of this conveniently fell into the decades of the Punch and Judy heyday: Phineas and his story were born.

There were unbelievable moments along the way. I discovered that the go-to expert on Punch and Judy history in Scotland only lived minutes away from me. I asked the Inverness Museum for permission to handle their Victorian Punch and Judy puppets and they said yes. And then, completely unexpectedly, I came across an 1890s picture of a dancing bear in Inverness. There was no way I couldn't include a dancing bear after that! And could I really pass up an opportunity to give Queen Victoria a cameo, especially when there were such detailed press records of her stay in Scotland that particular year?

Travelling with Phineas through Victorian Scotland has been a privilege, and telling his story in present tense and from his point of view has made him colourfully vivid in my imagination. My hope is that, despite the inevitable darker aspects of the story, this will be my readers' lasting impression, too.

As Charles Dickens himself put it in a letter to Mary Tyler in 1849: 'In my opinion the Street Punch is one of those extravagant reliefs from the realities of life.'

Wouldn't it be wonderful if, in a small way, my book could achieve the same?

ACKNOWLEDGEMENTS

I am immensely grateful to the many people who have made this book a reality. Thanks to:

Anne Glennie of Cranachan Publishing for believing in the book, for her insightful editing and for being such an unwavering champion of my writing. Corinna Bahr for the fantastic, eye-catching cover design. Martin MacGilp for his expert advice and assistance in all things Punch, and to Jamie Gaukroger of Am Baile for answering every question fully, no matter how eclectic.

Ross Wiseman for his hard work with the book trailer, Eden Court Creative for the use of their costumes and Inverness Museum for access to their beautiful Punch puppets. John Fulton for sourcing contemporary articles about Queen Victoria's 1889 Highland stay for me, and all #ClanCranachan authors being so incredibly supportive. The many book bloggers and readers who have got behind me, and all schools and book festivals who have supported my work by asking me to do events.

My fellow writers and SCBWI pals who cheer and chivvy me on my writerly way.

My friends, my church, my extended family: your excitement on my behalf means so much. And above all, Carla, Isla, Duncan and Rob, who have had to put up with a great deal on account of my writing, and still manage to be genuinely happy with me and for me. I love you all more than I can ever say.

God has blessed me with everything I could possibly need, and more.

Thank you.

About the Author

Barbara Henderson is the Inverness-based author of the critically acclaimed historical children's novel Fir for Luck, and is known for her energetic school events.

She splits her time between writing and teaching Drama to young people, but also volunteers on her local book festival committee.

Her house is home to one husband, three teenagers, a dog and a crazy collection of puppets.

Find out more about Barbara's writing at www.barbarahenderson.co.uk

Follow Barbara on Twitter @scattyscribbler

Also available in the Yesteryear Series

Fir for Luck

by Barbara Henderson

The heart-wrenching tale of a girl's courage to save her
village from the Highland Clearances.

Charlie's Promise

by Annemarie Allan

A frightened refugee arrives in Scotland on the brink of
WW2 and needs Charlie's help.

The Beast on the Broch

by John K. Fulton

Scotland, 799 AD. Talorca befriends a strange Pictish
beast; together, they fight off Viking raiders.

The Revenge of Tirpitz

by M. L. Sloan

The thrilling WW2 story of a boy's role in the sinking of
the warship Tirpitz.

Thank You for Reading

Pokey Hat publishes vibrant, imaginative and entertaining fiction titles, but we also want our readers to escape to Scotland by experiencing something of our exciting culture and history, wherever they live in the world.

We hope you enjoyed reading and sharing *Punch*, whether at school, at home, or cooried under the covers, and that it has brought the *story* in hi*story* to life.

Please tell all your friends and tweet us with your #Punch feedback, or better still, write an online review to help spread the word!

Find us online at

cranachanpublishing.co.uk

and follow us

@cranachanbooks

for news of our forthcoming titles.